Moon Over Gray Hills

Eric R. Ballein

"All children have to be deceived if they are to grow without trauma."

> -Kazuo Ishiguro,
> Never Let Me Go

"What does a scanner see? he asked himself. I mean, really see? Into the head? Down into the heart? Does a passive infrared scanner like they used to use or a cube-type holo-scanner like they use these days, the latest thing, see into me - into us - clearly or darkly? I hope it does, he thought, see clearly, because I can't any longer these days see into myself. I see only murk. Murk outside; murk inside. I hope, for everyone's sake, the scanners do better. Because, he thought, if the scanner sees only darkly, the way I myself do, then we are cursed, cursed again and like we have been continually, and we'll wind up dead this way, knowing very little and getting that little fragment wrong too."

> -Philip K. Dick,
> A Scanner Darkly

PROLOGUE

D ark swirls of black soot and ash rose into the midday sky, forming a cloud that slowly spun like the rotating arms of some far-flung galaxy. There was humming, swarms of locusts that had buried themselves deep in the ruined ground and embedded in the cracked walls of the surrounding buildings. Dilapidated foundations fell back into the earth, and roofs had caved into what were once living areas. Whatever else was still standing was broken and ransacked.

There were long-forgotten pieces of the miscellanea that we cultivate throughout our short lives. Shorter for those that had once lived there. Books and the shelves they once inhabited. Children's toys, dinnerware once shared among friends and families. Splayed out for all to see, a pillory of what once was and would never again be.

It was cold as Jonah stumbled, arms crossed in a feeble attempt at warmth, along the derelict streets. Everything around him looked blurry, like mountains viewed from a distance.

The air was difficult to breathe for the man no longer graced by youth. He moved slowly through the rubble, struggling to maintain his balance. Sandy blonde hair flew above him and swayed with the wind like a gently waving flag of surrender. Ash burned his eyes, and he kept blinking, hoping for relief, but it didn't come.

His vision was distorted and his mind as gray and murky as the water that rippled in puddles before him. The man tried to look for his reflection, but nothing stared back. Gray sludge just continued to churn in synchronized rotation with the sky above.

Every breath he drew became more difficult with each subsequent inhale that filled his barely-functioning lungs. They burned and strained to filter what little oxygen could be gleaned from the polluted and painfully cold air around him.

He paused for a moment., smelling something familiar that he couldn't quite place. *What is that?*

At first, it smelled of roasted pork. But he gagged and retched once he recognized it as the smell of burning flesh. His mind flashed morbidly back to the memory of a barbeque he had attended as a child. Or was it simply another dream?

"Here you go, honey. Now, grab a napkin and— listen to me, Jonah— don't spill anything on those pants. We just bought 'em for you, okay?"

It was a woman's voice. His mother's, he thought. But he couldn't recall any barbecues, nor could he make out his mother's face in the thick, blanketed fog of his memory. He could just hear her voice, soft and kind.

Then that vanished too.

When could it have been? Another life, perhaps. Another dream? Someone else's life or dream?

His throat constricted, and his breathing stuttered.

Holding a damp, dirty handkerchief he had pulled from his back pocket, he covered his mouth, intending to use it as a filter through which he could more easily breathe.

But the smell seemed to have rooted itself into the fabric as well as in his nose, painting every receptor with that nauseating scent.

It burned his nostrils, and tears streamed down his face, dancing around his chattering mouth. *What the hell is going on? All those people, just gone, in the—*

A low growling trembled in the distance, and the ground shook violently. There were tall gray buildings that shifted and fell with the ease of a sliding scale. As they fell, more dust rose to meet the ever-growing congregation that slowly spun above him.

He thought again of his mother or at least the image he held in his mind of what he perceived as his mother. All his thoughts and memories floated above him, an idea that remained forever beyond his grasp like so many other things — dancing in time with the looming sky above and the violent earth below.

There were old gospel songs he remembered hearing when he was a boy but couldn't pinpoint where he had heard them. This memory, like so many others for him, were untraceable in their origin. Yet, it was in his dreams where specific latent memories bubbled to the surface like an unconscious entity that waded just beyond the shallows of his mind.

The terror within Jonah grew. He stood, practically immobile, staring at that which had made the very earth beneath him quake. A large, black, dust-concealed mass with countless glowing eyes moved toward him. It groaned and whirred as it approached him with increasing speed. It's lumbering form casting a shadow that covered him completely.

He wanted to scream, to run, but he just stood there, stricken like a criminal whose head was already placed on the chopping block, the blade poised to fall.

The mass swung with the force of a great axe. He finally regained control of his body, backing up. It wasn't much, but it was the only action he could force his body to do. He didn't get far before he fell down the rim of an enormous crater, filled with rubble, dust, and bones.

This is it. This is the moment it all ends.

He held the handkerchief back to his mouth, breathing faster. All he could do now was watch. There was nowhere to run, nothing to do.

Like a pulsing swarm of cicadas, the mass descended on him.

CHAPTER 1

The whoosh of the automatic doors of the Jovial Fill-Up tore him away from his recollections — dark lines of sweat formed in patches on his bright blue uniform shirt. The dream, even in memory, was almost as terrifying to him now as it had been the night before. He could still feel the constriction of his chest, the futile grasping for breath, and the blur that only exists in the throes of terror.

It had felt so real. Different than any other dream I've ever had. The cold still lingered around him, moreso than usual.

The gas station clerk in his late-thirties rubbed his once bright eyes with the back of his hands. Stress lines spiderwebbed across his forehead, intermingling with the crow's feet accenting those same eyes.

Startled, he flinched at the sound of the doors opening. A young lady with long black hair tied into a bun walked into the fluorescent glow of the gas station. Jonah Downing smiled a fake customer service smile, but she was oblivious to him.

An attractive woman with chestnut skin and striking brown eyes, she wore a deep-gray jumpsuit, the uniform of the Factory just a couple of blocks away. The woman made for the cooler in large, graceful strides as he watched with cautious curiosity.

Everything Jonah did was with caution. He counted his steps home and would adjust his stride to compensate for an odd number (odd numbers were a bad sign, after all) and compulsively rechecked his oven and locks, sometimes running back home after already having left for work.

The woman grabbed a couple of cans of Factory beer and twirled around, catching the tail-end of Jonah's gaze as he shifted his eyes to anywhere else with awkward immediacy. *Shit, she saw me,* he thought as he pretended to take an interest in the gum placed near the register.

"Mint, spearmint, orange, mixed berry…" he softly spoke to himself as he looked over the packs with mock scrutiny. He squinted his eyes and counted on his fingers in a way that even a child could perceive as fiction.

"Everything there?" asked the woman with a voice that, despite its lilting timbre, had an authority that made Jonah startle.

Cheeks flushing scarlet, he looked up at her and feigned a laugh that he regretted instantly.

"Um… yeah, it seems so. I mean…um, we're missing a flavor, but-but I've made a note of that and will order it… tomorrow?"

"Which flavor are you missing?" she asked, eyeing the full rack of gum. There was not an open space to be seen. Jonah could feel a burning in his chest, and his palms were slick with sweat. Fingers filtered through his hair as he tried to think of a believable reply.

"Oh, well… I had already filled in the spot because

Mr.-Mr. Jacobs gets really cross with me if there's an open spot. He...um likes us to fill it in with another flavor— usually, spearmint since we have so much of it —and that's what I did. A-as you can see. He leaves this-this kind of stuff... to me." Jonah spoke in awkward spurts, periodically touching his hand to his forehead as if wiping sweat from his brow. *Actually,* wiping sweat from his brow.

Jonah, of course, was lying and had no actual authority here. Simply a gas station clerk, he did none of the ordering and none of the stocking, even. He just worked the register, cleaned the floors, and took out the trash.

He had been given some responsibility a few years back by Mr. Jacobs, directing the large tanker trucks from the Factory to the appropriate gas pumps in the station lot.

On his first day of receiving this new duty, Jonah was bursting with equal parts pride and apprehension. Downing was naturally a nervous man and spent a large amount of his time chewing at his thumb vigorously and pretending to smoke cigarettes. The latter was what he was doing when he forgot to hold his hand out, open-palmed, to signal the driver to stop. Instead, Jonah had watched helplessly as the tanker, reversing into its spot, hit the gas pump. Gasoline spewed forth from the severed machine, like blood from an amputated limb.

Mr. Jacobs had learned his lesson, and so had Jonah.

The woman smiled at him, either believing his lie or unwilling to address its falsehood. "Just these," she squinted her bright brown eyes as she read his nametag, "Jonah."

Jonah returned the smile bashfully and began scanning her purchases. He thought about what her life might be like outside of this exchange. She worked at

7

the Factory and was probably one of the employees who worked with the cargo ships coming to and from the moon. He wondered if she was one of the technicians who worked on the shuttles or if she just loaded up the supplies.

Maybe she worked in the indoor garden, cultivating mushrooms, carob, barley, cress, and various other plants that could survive indoors. The land was too infertile for most crops. He sometimes watched films at the Neon that mentioned the old farms, but it was hard to imagine now.

All the workers of the Factory wore the same jumpsuit, so distinguishing who did what was not an easy task. At least not for anyone who didn't work there.

Individuals were employed, no matter how inept they were, and given a place as a tool in the apparatus. A cog in the machine, or, in this case, a belt in the Factory.

Idyllic, almost to the point of utopian, Gray Hills had clear blue skies during the day and starry nights that left in awe those who took the time to look skyward. A better town could not be found for miles around, and if you asked any of the citizens, they wouldn't even be able to name another town.

The Factory was the pride of Gray Hills, the heart that was appropriately located at the center of the town. The most respected individuals in the city worked there, toiling away for the greater good of humanity. Or so it said in the radio broadcasts. The others who didn't work in the Factory did small jobs, like working at the gas station or the supermarket, though these were less respected positions.

Jonah had wanted to work at the Factory but couldn't pass the necessary tests required of him.

In those tests, different levels of aptitude were measured, including mental health, physical health, perceptiveness, and passion for the duty that the town had been so graciously afforded. He was always talking to himself, had a bad cough, his depth perception was subpar, and he had trouble keeping focused on any one task. Suffice to say, he did not fail by a small margin.

Yet, despite these shortcomings, the gas station clerk did have a fondness for words. He even scribbled bits of poetry when the mood struck him. Unfortunately, as it was not seen as a skill that could benefit the town, it was left unrefined and clandestine, forced to exist unseen in notebooks tucked beneath his mattress.

The woman in the Factory jumpsuit stared at him with a look he couldn't distinguish but that he had seen before. Her bright red lips were pursed, the bottom lip protruding, and her brow was knitted in frustration like it had been crafted by the angriest of hands.

"Hey, *Jonah*, can I get my bag or what?" said the girl in a wavering attempt to keep calm. He blinked, looked at the bag with her beverages still clutched in his hands, and blushed again.

"S-s-sorry about that, m-ma'am. You have a good day," stuttered Jonah as he handed over her purchase. She snatched it from his hands and stormed out of the automatic doors with an aggressive stride that still bore hallmarks of her prior grace.

It's true that Jonah didn't pass the perception tests required to work for the Factory, but he wasn't usually *this* absent-minded.

"It's that damn dream. It's messing with me. I can't th-think straight. Hell, I can't even speak right," he muttered shakily as he tapped his fingers in a simple rhythm on the laminated counter before him. He looked at his reflection, skewed and staring back at him. He didn't like what he saw.

Waiting for another customer, but knowing that it was well past the afternoon rush, he bided his time. If there was one thing Jonah did have, it was a modicum of

9

patience. It'd likely be another hour before he saw another soul step foot into the Jovial Fill-Up, and that would be Janet at the shift change.

Truthfully, he hated his job. The gas station clerk felt stuck, captured like an insect in amber, forced to live each moment by some unseen hand. His life was monotonous—mechanical—yet he was ashamed of these feelings.

He coughed and felt the satisfaction that came with it. He'd had a bad cough for a while now.

Jonah looked intently at his hands, at the rough and jagged tips of his fingers that were characteristic of a compulsive nail biter. They were unattractive as he stared at them, each one moving up and down in succession as they continued the rhythm.

The fingers abruptly stopped.

He saw something moving outside, a black figure—human it seemed—but covered entirely in what appeared to be a robe made of sackcloth. It was swiftly moving between two of the pumps on Jonah's left, darting between one pair and then another. Then it vanished from sight.

Jonah stepped from around the counter, out the automatic doors, and into the waning sunlight of the early evening. *What the hell was that,* he thought to himself as he breathed in the foul air that the Factory exuded. It vaguely reminded him of the smell in his dream. He felt nauseous all over again.

The dusk-approaching sky was a kaleidoscope of rose-tinted shades of blue and pink. He saw a cargo truck pass, from the supermarket in town, heading in the direction of the Factory.

The shuttles went to the moon twice a week, on Wednesdays and Sundays, to receive the supplies that were created in the Factory. Synthetic foods, usually canned or vacuum-sealed, were sent up along with clothes and various other essentials.

Jonah investigated the pumps where he had last seen the sackcloth figure, but there was nothing to see now. *Maybe they went around the station*, he thought as he moved back onto the sidewalk that traced the perimeter of the building.

The back of the Jovial Fill-Up was surprisingly pristine, with only a few discarded receipts and pieces of trash. Candy and artificial meat wrappers rolled back and forth like tumbleweeds in the early evening breeze. There was a large, brown dumpster with two plastic lids on the top of either side. Climbing up onto the step stool placed next to the dumpster, Jonah slowly lifted the lid closest to him and peered inside.

He saw nothing of the man- or thing- that he was looking for. There was just a dumpster half-filled with black plastic trash bags. The smell it exuded was an odd one, a combination of motor oil and horseradish. He turned around and leaned against the trashcan, awkwardly balancing himself on the stool.

Slapping his hands to his thighs as if to wipe them clean, he heaved a sigh of relief. Jonah then put two slightly parted fingers to his mouth as if he were smoking a cigarette. He took a fake drag, exhaled, and looked up at the moon.

It appeared to radiate, and the contours and craters looked magnificent even from his distant vantage. It was picturesque, almost to the point of seeming unreal, like a painting or a desert mirage.

He often imagined what it was like up there and occasionally found himself daydreaming about it. The train of thought would usually involve him stowing away or piloting a shuttle, making a new life for himself up there.

That was impossible, though.

Jonah exhaled as he closed the lid. There was

nothing there. *Maybe I'm losing my mind.* He stepped down from the stool.

Then, he noticed that the back door—only used when taking out the trash or escaping for cigarette breaks—was ajar.

His body tensed, and his knees buckled. He watched it swinging back and forth with the rhythm of the wind, creaking in alternating crescendos and diminuendos.

He moved toward the door, posture stilted and awkward. He had no idea what he'd do if he found it— whatever the hell *it* was. He had no weapon—hadn't even thought to grab the baseball bat under the counter on his way out—and he wasn't a particularly strong man.

Stupid, he thought. *So stupid.*

As the door blew open wide, he slipped through and tiptoed down the back hall, eyes shifting from the supply room to the employee lounge and back ahead to where the counter was.

Still nothing. Nothing out of place; no unusual shadows or foreign sounds.

He crept slowly to the counter and reached for the bat hidden under it. With the aluminum handle held tightly in his grasp, he felt a little safer.

Then, there was a squeak of feet on the tile floor. Jonah leaped with a yelp, dropping the baseball bat. It clanged loudly on the white tiled floor, and he stared helplessly down as it rolled away from him.

So goddamn close. It's always so goddamn close. His eyes darted frantically over the aisles.

"Running after ghosts again, Jonah?" asked an instantly recognizable voice. Its tone mocked the gas station clerk as he spun left. Standing beside the counter was his good friend Carlos Stultus, a reasonably handsome man with buzzed hair and a familiar dark-gray

Factory jumpsuit.

"Dammit, C-Carlos!" Jonah said between strained breaths. "You scared the sh… you scared me!"

He was Jonah's only friend, aside from Janet, and they had known each other for as long as he could remember. Then again, Jonah was often fuzzy on the finer details of his past. It all came to his mind in a a a cobble of blurry images. Calming a bit, he put his shaking hands in his pockets and tried to slow his breathing. "Wh-What're you doing here?"

"Other than scaring you shitless?" said Carlos as he chuckled at his own 'wit', seeming thoroughly amused by the situation. "Well, I actually came by to invite you to my place for dinner tonight." Carlos smiled wide, picking up a candy bar and setting it on the counter. A chocolate Factory Bar made from carob. Cocoa was a long-lost luxury. "What do you say?"

"Yeah, sure thing. Janet…" Jonah swallowed, moistening his dry mouth, "should be here to relieve me soon. Want me to bring anything?"

"Nah. And you can leave the bat, tough guy. I don't want you bringing round any trouble," Carlos teased. Jonah ignored him and began ringing up the candy bar.

Minutes later, he was shaking his head, watching his friend walk out of the station. Jonah was perplexed by the events that had been happening since last night. Or this morning, depending on how you were keeping track.

First, there was the dream. Now the figure between the gas pumps. *It's gotta be a coincidence. Two weird events,* he thought as he looked down at the counter.

Or maybe there's a connection between them.

Before him on the counter was a book—one that had not been there when he left to investigate the pumps. Or at least he had not remembered seeing it there.

Memory was a fickle enterprise, especially for him. For the whole town.

Jonah picked it up, stuffed it quickly into his backpack beneath the counter, and anxiously waited for Janet to come in and relieve him of his shift. His eyes darted from his bag to the front doors and behind him.

Just another hour or two, he thought. *Not much longer now.*

Then what? An answer to the question? The book, the dream, the figure? Unlikely. Even he wasn't foolish enough to believe that.

"How was your day?" she asked him, pulling her long golden hair up into a ponytail. Janet was short and a little heavier set, but all the more beautiful for it.

"It was... was okay," he said. He didn't want to go into what had happened. Not with her. She wasn't very understanding when it came to things that couldn't easily be explained. Janet was of a mind that things either were, or they weren't. There weren't many shades of gray in her book, at least concerning the supernatural. Or paranormal. Or whatever the hell this was.

And if it was all just a hallucination? He didn't want to test those waters either. Not yet. But he might tell her, eventually. She was his friend, after all. One of only a few.

"Well, you're free to go. Got any plans tonight?" She placed herself next to Jonah, crossing her arms and leaning on the counter. He found her very attractive but could never tell her so. They had been friends for too long, and he dreaded the idea of making her feel awkward or uncomfortable.

She was a stubborn woman, headstrong and overly honest, sometimes to Jonah's detriment. At times, he felt that she was the living antithesis of himself. And, in a way, that's what drew him to her.

"Dinner with Carlos and Margaret. You?" he said.

She smiled wryly, her round face adorned with two dimples as she waved her arms around the counter. "Stuck here for the night. Obviously," she added, touching her nametag.

"Oh, yeah. That... that should've been obvious," Jonah said. He felt drained all of a sudden, overwhelmed by the occurrences of the day.

"Okay, well, get out of here before I have security throw you out!" she said with mock authority. "And, in case you didn't know," she whispered, "I'm security."

He laughed, grabbed his backpack and began to move toward the door, hands in the air. "All right, all right. I don't want any trouble. Have a good night."

"You too," she said, and the cool evening air enveloped him once more as he walked out of the automatic doors.

CHAPTER 2

Jonah sat on an old leather lounge chair in the living room of the Stultus residence. Carlos had gone upstairs to change into more comfortable clothes, and Carlos's wife Maggie was still at the supermarket with their son, Oliver. Jonah took a few glances around to make sure no one was going to interrupt him, then slowly took out the book that he had carefully stuffed into his backpack earlier that day.

It was an old thing; a black leather-bound tome that looked as though it had been around for decades. Covered in thick layers of dirt and ash, it was a large book that was even more cumbersome than it looked—almost like it was made of lead.

The spine was weak and tattered from several thousand readings. The pages were aged yellow, the text appearing grayish, rather than the crisp black it once was. It smelled of mildew and sulfur and... something else. A distinct musk. It must have been with the same person for a long time. So long that their smell had embedded itself into the leather binding.

Jonah wiped some dirt from the cover to make out the faded title in a golden script; *All Things are Nothing.* He opened it, hoping to discover a publication date or the author's name but found neither. All he saw, scrawled in black ink, were the initials A.S.

Could they be the author's initials? Or maybe they were the previous owner's initials written in case they'd lost their book. He pondered each possibility and mouthed out possible names.

"Alice Smith. Alexander Stewart. Avery Scott..." he went on for a minute or two as he flipped through the musty pages, but abruptly stopped when something grabbed his attention. His mouth, still open, began to mouth along as he read the words on page thirty-nine:

Our worlds come crumbling down around us in the blink of an eye. The world itself, wrought with hatred and strife, literally succumbed to the most significant loss our Mother has ever felt. We hate those bombs, those harbingers of destruction, but should we?

I'd hate to think that any light with such brilliance, thousands of times brighter than our sun, is evil. It can't be malicious, not really. It is power. The latent potential of such a thing cannot be blamed on the bombs, but rather on the men and women who misuse them.

Instead, maybe we should love them. Grudges harbor cancer in our hearts that can't be cured by any kind of radiation.

It's true, the bombs left devastation in their wake, but isn't it the suffering of those closest to us that opens our eyes?

If you're reading this, you're different. You survived. And, whether you know it or not, you have a purpose. We don't worship the bombs, or people, or the past. We worship the opportunity for a clean slate. You will undoubtedly know this in your heart of hearts…

A key in the front door startled Jonah back to reality, and he quickly stuffed the book back into his bag.

Jonah sprang up to help Maggie and Oliver with the groceries, grabbing three bags and a container of purified water and carried them into the kitchen. He gingerly set them on the counter next to the refrigerator and turned to Maggie, flashing a weak smile. She didn't look like she was in a good mood, but he felt compelled to initiate small talk, regardless of her feelings. This was a flaw of Jonah's, one that he was aware of but felt compulsively pulled to, nonetheless. *Like the cart to the horse,* or however that saying went.

"How was your day, Maggie? Mine was pretty interesting. You know that—" but Maggie lifted her hand to silence Jonah.

"You talk too much, Jonah. Goddamn. You ramble on and on and…" She drew a sharp breath and let out a sigh. "My day was okay. Some things… came up that I had to deal with, but everything will be alright now."

Jonah nodded, fearful of speaking too much. He knew that she wasn't trying to be rude to him; merely frank. In everything Jonah discussed, he would beat around a point, talking and talking before ever getting there. The gas station clerk knew better than to take offense.

It wasn't uncommon for him to forget the initial

point entirely. He actively tried to be more direct and ramble less, but old habits were hard to break. They pulled him down with considerable gravity, and he was unsure of how to rise back up afterward. It was often easier just to lay where he was.

She started to put synthetic milk substitute and cheese-product into the fridge as he idly watched her. Then, realizing that he should probably do something other than just standing around, he walked toward the counter where the rest of the groceries were placed.

"Um… do you need any help?" Silly question. Carlos would have known to help rather than asking if it was needed, but Jonah wasn't aware of the nuances of domestic life.

She looked up at him, seemingly surprised by the request, and then smiled a little. Just a little. "Sure. Can you put the canned stuff away?" She pointed to the far side of the kitchen. "In the cupboard."

He nodded and got to work, placing dozens of cans of mushrooms, endive, and carrots into uniform rows on the bottom shelf of the large cupboard. He had just finished throwing the empty brown paper bags into the recyclables when Carlos walked into the kitchen.

His friend was now wearing old jeans, a white T-shirt with a light red stain on the chest, and a denim jacket that was at least one size too small. He went over to his wife, put his arms around her from behind in a tender embrace, and softly kissed the back of her head.

Jonah desperately longed for that kind of intimacy, but as he often did with most feelings, he shook it away.

The gas station clerk turned his gaze over to Oliver who was handling a small, round object. He had been intently examining it since he had gotten home. The boy's sullen eyes looked at it with curiosity and… was it fear?

"What've you got there?" Jonah asked. Oliver

shrugged his thin shoulders dismissively. The boy was sixteen but had a small frame for his age. One could describe him by his likeness to a pole or a thin stick, and they wouldn't be exaggerating as much as you'd think.

The boy's hair was a light brown but would likely turn darker as he matured to be more like his father's. He was only five-two, a rather skinny and short young man —in this way quite unlike his father, who was tall and broad.

"I'm not sure," he murmured through thin lips only a shade darker than his pale skin. The boy met Jonah's eyes. They drooped with apparent exhaustion. Oliver was an odd sight, Jonah realized; obviously the youngest in the room but also appearing older in some undefinable way.

The boy also had a persistent cough that only seemed to be getting worse. Anytime Jonah tried mentioning it to Carlos, he'd just dismiss it as though it was something temporary, a young man under the weather. But children weren't often 'under the weather' for several months straight.

Had it really been that long?

He looked up at Jonah then went back to staring at the object he held. He was not amused, and his pallid face looked even less so when paired with his thin, crooked frown.

"It's probably nothing," said the boy with indifference. Jonah looked at the object closer and finally realized what it was.

"It's a… rock?"

The boy sighed. "Yeah, but look closer at it. It's not like the rocks we find around town." He outstretched his hand to show Jonah the stone.

It was grayish-blue and seemed to glisten in the light of the room. Jonah reached out to brush his fingers against it lightly; It was surprisingly smooth. Small slivers of green quartz within gleamed even brighter than the surface, strewn haphazardly about the body of the stone.

"I've never seen anything like it," he said, marveling at the slick surface, the alien beauty it held. "Where did you find it?"

"Out front of the school. I got there early, like I usually do, and found it sitting on the steps. It had a note taped to it," the boy said.

"What did it say?"

The boy hesitated for a moment. "It just said… *Everything is Nothing*. Pretty weird, right?"

A pang of apprehension rattled Jonah from the inside out. *Everything is Nothing;* the same as the book. On the same day as the dream and the figure. Like the others, it could be nothing, but… Jonah tried to recall an old saying about stacking coincidences and what that meant. The saying eluded him.

He pointed to the rock. "Do… you mind if I hold it?" His voice wavered slightly. Oliver took one last glance at the stone in his hand and set it down on the table.

"Sure. You can have it," he said. "It creeps me out."

Jonah grabbed the rock, feeling its full weight in his hands for the first time. Like the book, it was heavier than it first appeared. Leaving the kitchen, he went back to the chair by the front door and placed it into his backpack.

When he returned, food was being dished out by Carlos as Maggie and Oliver patiently waited in their seats. Jonah helped Carlos finish up and then took his spot at the space adjacent from his friend.

Carrots and Synth Meat made from mushrooms had been combined into some kind of casserole. It did not look appetizing, but it tasted alright—at least to Jonah. No one commented one way or the other. He smiled, but the rest didn't, so he let his mouth fall back into place.

They ate in relative silence, but after the dishes had been cleared, Carlos and Maggie began to talk about their respective days.

"… Yeah, I had this huge order I had to put into one of those shuttles today," Carlos said. "Damn colonists need almost twice what they were getting a year ago, but we have fewer people doing the work! And—cover your ears, Ollie—the fuckers're paying us the *same damn amount*." Carlos sighed and leaned back in his chair—it creaked beneath the weight. Oliver rolled his eyes and shook his head at the mention of the curse word that he had definitely *not* covered his ears for.

Margaret watched her husband with a mixture of fondness and disapproval. "Listen, hon, I know that things have been getting difficult, but you've got to remember why you're doing this. For the greater good, the betterment of humankind. Those brave souls up there depend on us. They depend on you."

"Yeah, I know, but I just—" But before he could finish, his wife aggressively broke in.

"You need to get over it. Dammit, Carlos!" The fondness was gone, the disapproval lingered. "You know they can't manufacture enough up there to sustain themselves—not yet. So, do your work, stop bitching, and be happy it's worth something." At this last bit, she darted her eyes toward Jonah to drive the point home. Her husband worked in the Factory, and Jonah worked in a gas station. As a clerk.

Jonah noticed this silent attack on his character but knew better than to say anything about it. He wasn't always a fool.

Carlos raised his hands in submission. "But how long have we been doing this, Maggie?"

"What do you mean?", she asked.

"I mean, I can't remember when this started. When

we began this—" he gestured his hands in front of him, grasping for the words "—business with the Factory. The moon. The colonists. Do you remember Maggie? Because I don't."

Silence fell around the table. She looked down at her feet, as did Jonah. Oliver just stared blankly at his father.

Now aware of the awkwardness of the situation, and realizing some issues are best left unresolved, Carlos decided to change the subject.

"Anyway... do you want to see a movie tomorrow, Jonah? Maggie was telling me about... what was it again?"

Margaret's face brightened a little. "Oh yeah, it's this interesting film called *Bitter Wine*. Or, I hear it's interesting. My friend Nancy was telling me about it at work today. It's supposed to be about, like, some kind of deserted town where the people have all died from poison, or exposure, or something like that."

"Really?" asked Jonah.

"Yeah, it's supposed to be some art film or something. It was shot as though it had really happened. Minimal editing, difficult to hear voices. Apparently, they really committed to the bit. They wanted it to seem really", she grasped for the word, "realistic."

She paused, took a drink of water, then continued.

"That's what Nancy said, anyway. It's supposed to be a new film, and I haven't seen a new film since..." Her voice trailed off as she tried to recall when that was. Her look became absent, probably reaching into her mind, into the dark caverns of her memory, but retrieved nothing.

The room was oddly silent once again. Jonah couldn't remember the last time a new film had come to the town theater either, but then again, he couldn't remember a lot of things. Especially today. Yet, as he sat there shuffling in his chair, he wondered if this was yet another connection he could make—another coincidence. *How many were there now?*

"Hey, why don't you come with us, Jonah? We'd love to have you along," said Carlos. Maggie maintained her smile and nodded in agreeance. "It'll be a great time. You can even invite Janet if she's not working."

Jonah's interest was piqued by the odd movie description and its possible relation to what had been happening to him. Yet, he was unsure of whether he should go. He realized that it could further feed his anxieties, exacerbating them to a point that... well, he was scared of.

"I'd love to," he replied.

#

Later that evening, he arrived back at his small home; a sparsely furnished building that was always colder than he liked. It had cracked windows, covered corner to corner in spiderwebs of both fine silk and fractured glass. Dust gathered thickly on the few pieces of furniture that he owned. His cupboard was full of cans of synthetic beef hash, and the refrigerator was perpetually empty. He had long since abandoned the habit of staring into its empty yellow light, wishing for fresh food to appear.

The gas station clerk stared out the squat window placed awkwardly in the corner of his kitchen. Wiping away the thick layer of dust that had accumulated there since the last night, he marveled at the sky. The moon shone brightly, and the stars twinkled bashfully. It all looked so beautiful to him; the only ideal thing he knew to be universally true.

I could use more truth in my life, especially today.

His room, or rather, the place that he slept in, was

more like a closet. The sole objects occupying its shoebox space were a plastic dresser, a clothes hamper, and a mattress. The latter of which sat on the floor, taking up most of the room.

He turned on the radio and listened to the evening update. A sharp and brassy male voice spoke excitedly:

"Don't fret, citizens of Gray Hills. Your hard work is being taken into account, and we, up above, genuinely appreciate your hard work. You're toiling for the greater good of humanity. All great things involve considerable risk, as I'm sure you well know. But fear not, for soon—yes, very soon—you will be exalted with us. Think not of the future but of the moment. Here and now, men and women. Here and now. You're different, all of you. We've survived because of you. This is your purpose."

Jonah lay, blankly staring at the water-stained ceiling. The broadcast reminded him of something... but what?

The book. They weren't exactly the same, but the book and the broadcast contained the same message. The same message that we, the vaguely defined audience, were different. And that means... what exactly?

On that mattress where he now laid, Jonah clutched his backpack in his arms. He had not changed his clothes or even attempted to clean himself; he just stayed there, anticipating the following evening.

He wondered about the book and why it appeared to him. Him, of all people. And as he laid there wondering, his head throbbed, and his vision began to blur — likely just the stress of the day.

Jonah tried to sleep—but sleep eluded him. He would close his eyes for a few minutes, systematically tensing and releasing different muscles in his body in an attempt to coax rest into coming. After two hours of failed attempts, he surrendered and resigned himself to, once again, staring at the ceiling.

That stain, black and brown, looked like an inkblot test he had seen therapists use in old movies. What did he see? A man? Maybe a beetle? Maybe—

A low-voice down the hall startled him.

Jonah's eyes widened, and his heart rate spiked, but he did not move. He just focused on the voice, trying to discern a level of comprehension from the alien sound. The voice stopped suddenly, and he slowly turned his head to the open doorframe.

A figure stood there, silhouetted by the blackness around and behind it. It stepped forward, and Jonah's body was unmoving as it closed the distance between them. He closed his eyes, hoping to whisk away the figure by not looking at it, but it drew nearer nonetheless.

He felt its breath now, soft warm exhales that bristled the hairs on his neck and left goosebumps cascading down his back. The voice, now discernibly female, spoke softly in his ear with a smoothness that struck him as familiar. As comforting.

"The sun became black as sackcloth; the full moon became like blood."

"W-what?" he murmured almost inaudibly.

She repeated, "The sun became black as sackcloth; the full moon became like blood."

He opened his eyes and could see the figure was thin and almost formless. Any feature that should have been easy for him to make out at such a small distance was just as shrouded as when it stood on the threshold.

"Remember this, when you discover the true shape

of things," it said.

Jonah blinked hard, closing his eyes and trying to calm his shaking breath.

When he reopened his eyes, she had dissipated, like a fog illuminated by the morning sun.

All through the night, she did not return, and Jonah entirely gave up on the prospect of sleep. The radio buzzed, and white noise filled the gaps of silence it left behind.

A stack of coincidences is no longer an exercise of chance. That was the saying he had almost remembered earlier. He repeated it like a mantra until sunlight broke through the evening dark and put an end to the long and sleepless night.

CHAPTER 3

J onah shuffled in his chair, anxious at the thought of what this film would entail. He reached down to touch his backpack on the floor, a reassurance of his sanity. It was proof that at least some things happening existed in the physical realm and not in his possibly cracked mind.

There was only one theater in town, a filthy and cramped little place called the Neon. It had a busted sign and served snacks that were perpetually stale and overpriced.

Jonah felt for the shape of the book and sat back up to see Janet staring at him.

"Did you... forget something, Jonah?" she said.

"Oh, uh... well... no. I thought that I had, which is- is why I checked, but it turns out I have it," he said.

"What were you afraid you were missing?"

"I was worried..." Jonah paused a moment, trying to formulate a passable lie. "That I forgot—" but before he could finish, the lights in the theater dimmed, and the projector whirred. *Thank god*, he thought to himself, and turned to her to whisper, "I'll tell you later." She smiled back and gave him a look that he could discern, one that he hated to see. It was what she called her 'that's bullshit' face.

Goosebumps rose on his arms, and his stomach was a tangled knot of apprehension. He closed his eyes, imagining some vertigo-like sensation would come over him at any moment, but when he opened his eyes, the movie title appeared on the large black screen in bold white letters.

The Time Machine, the film based on the book of the same name, was playing. He blinked to make sure his eyes hadn't deceived him. Jonah had distinctly remembered seeing *Bitter Wine* displayed on the small marquis out front of the theater.

Jonah turned toward Maggie, who sat two seats away from him with Carlos in between. He whispered, "What happened to the movie you were telling me about? The new one. With the town, the consumption, or whatever it was."

Maggie seemed confused and shrugged. "I don't know. I saw the sign, and like I said last night, Nancy told me about it. I doubt it's some kind of grand conspiracy." She smiled at the joke she had made, but Jonah didn't find it very funny. *It just might be.* "Do you think we should ask an employee?"

"I'll do it," said Jonah as he began to stand up and push toward the aisle. The film had already started, and people were glaring at him as he awkwardly maneuvered past the half-dozen spectators that sat between him and the nearest exit.

He pushed passed the double doors of the theater out into the blindingly bright lobby, rapidly blinking to adjust to the drastic difference. Jonah walked up to a small counter opposite the doors where a young woman slumped, looking bored. She glanced up at him, raising her posture slightly, and gave him a weak but kind enough smile. As he got closer, he saw that her name tag read Alice.

"Hello, sir. Did you want some snacks? Maybe a Factory Bar?" said the young woman gesturing toward the smudgy display case beneath her. There were several candy bars and mushroom 'meat' sticks and various other snacks encased behind the grease-stained glass. "Or maybe a soda?"

"No… I… but thanks. I was um… was wondering what happened to the movie that was supposed to be playing. You know, *Bitter Wine*, I think it's called."

She blinked a couple of times as if trying to comprehend what it was that he was asking. Then her eyes flashed with some vague recognition.

"Ah… yeah. Well, that film was taken out of the rotation for seeming too…"she struggled to find an adjective and shrugged. "It really bothered some people who saw it. One guy in particular demanded we take it down."

Jonah blinked. "But… it's still advertised on the—"

"Yeah, I know. Sorry, but there's nothing that can be done about it. You can talk to my manager if you'd like," she said.

"Is your manager here?" he asked.

"No."

Of course not, he thought, but didn't say. "Well… what'll happen to the movie?"

"That's not up to me. Sorry." She shrugged, then seeing how much her answer seemed to affect him, she added, "But I can give you information on who brought the film to us in the first place… if you want." Before waiting for a reply, she turned her head from left to right, flipped over a theater poster to its glossy white back-side, and began to write in her most legible script.

Alice handed the poster slowly to Jonah. It was as if she was unsure whether she should be giving this kind of information to a stranger. *She probably shouldn't be, but I'll take any bit of help I can get. Any piece of information that could possibly illuminate what exactly is going on.*

"He left the information with us to give to anyone asking about it," Alice said as she handed it to him.

Jonah looked at it and saw the vague script written: *Farris. 1433 High Street.*

He felt an urge to ask, 'Is that all?' but fought against it. This was better than nothing. Anything was better than nothing.

"Thank you," he said as he rolled the poster into a tight cylinder and put it into the pocket of his jacket.

Pushing through the glass doors to the brisk evening outside, he felt calmer now. The night air was chilly, and it felt good to breathe it in.

Jonah began to pace back and forth on the sidewalk in front of the Neon. Pacing always helped him think. He began listing the occurrences in his head in order, muttering stray words here and there like quiet confessions in a casino chapel.

First, there was the nightmare. Then the figure at the gas station. Then the book. Then the rock. Maggie talked about a movie, a new film, and no one can remember the last time that happened. Finally, this movie was affecting people so much that it was pulled from the Neon—quickly—by someone. Who? And that means...

Means what? He wanted to form some grand connection between these events, to unravel some glaring conspiracy concealed just beneath the surface. He just needed to find the loose thread, he thought—then it would all come undone.

But his mind felt dull, exhausted from sleep

deprivation and obsession.

He wanted to try to work it out with someone. Or, at the very least, just talk to someone about it. But he needed to wait until he had something real, something substantial to prove it. Jonah pulled the poster back out, unrolled it and examined it once again.

I've never heard of High Street, he thought, *and I've lived in this town for as long as I can remember. Which has been for how long again? I'll look at a map tomorrow.*

Jonah coughed loudly, covering his mouth with a tightly balled fist. He felt a pain in his chest, like the slowly burning fire of a muted flame. Spitting on the ground, he saw blood. Wiping his mouth with his jacket sleeve, he chose not to think about what that meant. There was no time for that now.

An ache at the base of his skull pushed relentlessly, a throbbing pressure that made a kaleidoscope of bright lights swim around him. He closed his eyes and took a deep breath, counting back from ten, then let the air slowly deflate his lungs.

The pain had cleared some, leaving only the edges of his vision blurred. He began to put away the poster when he saw movement out of the corner of his eye.

Beneath a streetlamp in the parking lot of the Neon, about a hundred yards away, Jonah saw it—whatever it was—bending over and standing back up in repetition. It was like a machine, forming the same action with exact precision over and over again. The creature was a giant, humanoid insect, beetle-like in appearance. He approached it slowly, trying to get a better glimpse of what it was he was looking at.

It can't be real. Maybe it's a trick of the light. Maybe—

Its thorax was large, moving up to form slanted peaks above its head, and its arms were sharp scythes, several feet in length. The beetle's exoskeleton was jet black with shards of blue that shone green at certain angles. There were no wings that Jonah could see, but its back was lost in the shadows outside of the spotlight.

With a little more speed, Jonah continued forward, too curious to process the fear he should be feeling. His shoes tapped softly onto the cracked concrete of the parking lot as he moved closer, sending back weak echoes of sound.

Jonah could now see why it was leaning over and standing up; it was eating.

The remnants of a small animal were laid out in front of the insect, blood pooling on the black canvas of the parking lot around its legs. It had been mutilated past the point of recognition, and Jonah couldn't decide whether it had been a cat, dog, or raccoon. Maybe it was none of these. Whatever it had been, it was nothing now.

The creature had thin slits of glowing eyes on its small tilted head. They settled on Jonah, and its feelers rose to attention. It stood still for a moment, slowly brought itself upright as if ready to strike, and dashed toward him with great speed. Its antennae began flailing about wildly, and its pincers clacked like a cadence of drumsticks.

Jonah stuffed the poster back into his pocket, turned and ran. His eyes were fixed on the glass door of the theater as he sprinted with every ounce of energy he had. He wanted to look back, to see how close it was gaining on him, but fought the urge.

He tried to ignore everything around him as he made for the door, his singular and only focal point, but he could still hear its clacking. It was getting louder now, and faster. He could feel the displacement of air as it rushed toward him, so close now.

Will I be a corpse on the ground? Blood and body indiscernible from the man I used to be?

The creature made a low gurgling sound that sounded vaguely like a growl. Its pincers clicked faster until there was almost no space between the subsequent strikes.

Making it to the porch of the theater, Jonah swung the door open as hard as he could and crossed the threshold of the lobby, bent over with his hands on his knees. He was heaving in front of the concession stand, Alice watching him with a mix of horror and curiosity. She opened her mouth as if to speak, then paused as she saw him opening his mouth. Trying his best to form words.

"Look out there... do... d-d-do you see it?" He managed between gasps. Alice looked at him with uncertainty and then looked out the window. She stood on tip-toes, tilted her head, staring for a good while as if scrutinizing something hidden among the shadows of the one streetlight. She moved her head left, then right.

"There's... nothing there..." she said when she looked back at him, pity apparent in her voice. Jonah darted up, looked out the window himself, and saw nothing but the parking lot and the street lamp. Its dim light trickled down on the space beneath it, but there was nothing there. No creature. No dead animal. Not a drop of dark blood.

He wanted to explain, to detail the terrifying contours of all that he had just encountered but thought better of it. Jonah knew this girl was long past the point of believing anything he could say.

Alice began to speak again, but he couldn't hear her words, just the patronizing tone of them. Jonah started toward the double doors of the theater, ignoring the woman at the counter. Sweat dripping down and accumulated on the small of his back. His face felt numb and tingled like a tongue on a low-voltage battery.

The film was still playing, and Jonah, deciding to

stay near the doors so he wouldn't interrupt anyone, made a conscious effort to quiet his breathing. He'd had enough judgmental glares from strangers for one night.

On the screen, an all too familiar scene was playing out, the only part of the film that had ever really stood out to him.

He watched through the eyes of the time traveler as the moon fell apart. Jagged lines cut across it, breaking off in large chunks as debris rained down on the city, crushing vehicles and collapsing buildings. Detritus landed on unsuspecting people in the background, scrambling vainly away.

He felt as though he had already lived through a disaster, albeit in the form of a dream. And how had he reacted in that dream? Like an open-mouthed child gaping absently at that which he could never hope to stop.

CHAPTER 4

O nce again, Jonah stood behind the counter of the Jovial Fill-Up. His eyes had dark rings beneath them, and red-tinted lines surrounded his irises like flashes of lightning. The gas station clerk looked rough and felt worse. His mind felt like a torrent of images and fears that he couldn't even begin to organize, let alone categorize.

I've got one foot in this world and another somewhere else, he thought. *Or maybe it's a veil that's been lifted and that I can't seem to adjust to.*

It didn't matter.

All that mattered was that he was stuck there, caught between the life he had known and the life that he was experiencing now — torn in half between the two.

Earlier that day, he had shown the book to Janet, proving its existence in the physical realm to another set of eyes. There was that. They had sat around his small kitchen table as he held it up in one vigorously shaking hand, unknowingly decrying his sanity in the process.

"Do-do you see this, Janet? Goddammit, tell me you see it", he said, voice tremulous with fear.

"Well, I see a book. Is that... what you see?" she asked cautiously, fighting the beginnings of a wry smile. She must've thought Jonah was joking, but he ignored it and pressed on.

"Thank god," he murmured. "Thank god."

"Is that why you called me over here? Because if so, Jonah, that's pretty batshit even for you," she said. Her voice hovered a line between concern and jeer.

"No! Well, yes. Partly. But not exactly. This book is important. There's been all of this... stuff happening. It's all muddled. I um... wasn't sure if this book was even real," he said with manic expression, arms waving violently before him in an arcing ellipse of motion.

"Janet, you have no idea what I've been through. I-first, I had this dream. Then I saw something out in front of the gas station- I went out to investigate it- and there was nothing. *Nothing*. Then, I came inside, and this book was sitting on the counter. Just there! And then, you know when we went to the movies?" Janet nodded, eyes wide. "Well, when I went outside- wait! First, I thought the movie that was supposed to play was going to be important. Like, connected. I don't know how; it was just another weird thing. An unexplainable feeling. Anyway, I went out to check *why* the movie was pulled, I got a poster and- and then I went outside, and I saw this huge fucking beetle-monster eating this..."

"Stop!" she said, eyes wet with tears now. "Just stop. Jonah, I can't help you. Whatever is wrong with you is way out of my realm of expertise." She stood, shaking her head. She forced herself to look at him pityingly. "You've got some problems. You're a fucking shitshow. And I-I can't take it anymore. I just can't." And with this, she ran out of the kitchen. He heard the front door slam behind her, leaving him alone. She had left, and the hope of sharing his burden left with her.

He now stood hunched over a map that he had stolen from the shelf next to the kitschy paperweights and news programs that no one ever bought.

It was spread out before him, creased edges unevenly placed throughout, and he was keenly inspecting it. Throughout the entire town of Gray Hills, there was no sign of a High Street. He had, at this point, looked at every street three times over. Nothing.

In the rare case that a customer came in during his investigation, Jonah would swiftly ring up the customer's items and get them out as quickly as possible. Then, vainly determined, he would pick up where he left off.

Although there was no sign of High street, Jonah did notice an unnamed road in an uninhabited area in the northwest corner of the town. He had never been there and had only seen the end of Elm Street that was, according to the map, next to that unnamed street. But there was nothing after Elm street, just empty roads leading out of Gray Hills and desert wilderness. To places beyond? Elm street itself had been evacuated and left in disrepair some years before. He couldn't remember the exact number.

"Why would there be an unnamed area on an official map?" he muttered to himself in disbelief. None of this added up, and he, hoping to gain some foothold of what it was that was happening, only discovered more gears to a machine that he couldn't possibly hope to understand.

His life felt like a never-ending set of nesting dolls, always revealing another and another and then another still.

Jonah felt now that it was quite likely, especially after the events of the night before, that he was unstable. Even Janet thought so.

You're a fucking shitshow, she had said. Maybe

Janet was right.

He could have possibly contrived some way to convince himself that every other part of this had some tangible connection to reality. But, when a giant insect chases you, and no one else can see it, the situation is a far cry from any semblance of sanity.

But he couldn't stop thinking about it. If, by some ridiculous and improbable means, this truly was happening, he had to find out why. It was the only thing he could hold onto. It was exponentially better than the alternative, a final straw he had to grasp for. If not this, then what?

A tremor moved through him, a chill that ran from his head and outstretched itself to the tips of his fingers. Goosebumps flickered and tingled. He felt fear, pure terror, at the questions posed. He tore the map into pieces, screaming at the emptiness around him. The gas station clerk threw it away and took a deep breath.

For the first time since he had gotten to the station, Jonah decided to focus his attention on the tasks of the job rather than his gnawing preoccupations with the events prior.

The store, slower than usual, forced him to search for miscellaneous distractions by which to focus his unspent energy. He wiped down the counter with sanitizer, swept the floors of the lobby, and stocked what little could be stuffed into the already full coolers and shelves: alcoholic drinks and canned foods, mostly.

Gathering his things, Jonah glanced to make sure no one was in the gas station, more out of compulsion than necessity, and began to collect trash. He went into both bathrooms, reeking of cleaning alcohol and urine. With gloved hands, Jonah dumped the waste into a large black plastic bag. He did the same with the garbage out front and in the break room, tied the bag up in a double-knot, and stepped out the back door toward the large dumpster.

He opened the lid on his left and swung the large bag over his head and into the bin, hitting the other bags as plastic-against-plastic rustled on contact.

Downing closed the lid, leaned against the back wall, and mimed smoking a cigarette. He brought the index and middle finger of his right hand, slightly parted, up to his lips as he slowly pretended to take a drag.

Jonah had never been a smoker, but in times of stress, he found peace in imitating the act. It was an odd thing for him, something the people around him did, but not something he could ever bring himself to stomach. And, despite never taking to the habit, he had a phlegm riddled, chest-rattling cough as if he had been smoking for years.

The cough had developed itself two years before. One morning, when he had tried to sit up from his bed, his effort was promptly halted by a small coughing fit. At the time, he had thought that maybe he was coming down with a cold or some other illness, but the cough persisted.

The back of Jonah's head pulsed with a disorienting pain that buckled his knees. He clenched his fists and took a deep breath through his nose, slowly let it out through gritted teeth. It seemed to help, if only a little.

Momentarily calmed, Downing pretended to take another drag when, while looking up to the sky, he stopped his miming gesture. His hands fell to his side, and his mouth began to move rapidly as if he were talking, but no sound escaped his lips.

The sky, in a matter of moments, had transformed from its prior serene shades of blue to something else entirely. Where there were shadows cast from the afternoon sun, the whole sky itself seemed an ominous shadow. The sky was a dark, powdery gray that seemed to be a mixture of dust, soot, and ash. It checkered the air in a variety of shades that ranged from off-white to jet black.

The sun, once an apparent truth of the sky, ceased to exist. Yet, the moon still hung over Gray Hills, but it was no longer a radiant pearl in the sky. It looked darker now, menacing, and Jonah felt fear grip his chest painfully.

It's just like my dream, he thought. *It's just like my dream, it's just- it's just- it's;* his mind continued as if it were a skipping vinyl on a damaged record player.

A faint glow started to appear at the four corners of the sky, and a tremendous and capricious breeze blustered around him. It was so forceful that it almost knocked him over, and he gasped in response to the displaced air. The wind, initially seeming to come from multiple directions, converged and circled around him, forming a small whirlwind of trash and gravel.

The smell of acrid smoke hung thickly on the air like a dark curtain waiting to fall. Jonah began to back up against the wall of the station as the wind picked up momentum. A piece of glass from a discarded coffee mug hit Jonah square on his left cheek and left a deep gash. Blood slowly seeped down his face like honey spilling from an upturned mason jar.

There was a sound coming from around the corner of the gas station wall. It was the slow and steady scraping of something dragging against the stone ground. Jonah looked towards the sound, back pressed against the wall, and saw a black head peering from around the corner with glowing red eyes that burned like the embers of a flickering fire.

Those eyes blinked and stared. There were no pupils or sclera, just an all-consuming iris — with dancing shades of red and orange.

That smell was there again, like a pig roasting on a

spit. *That damn smell*, he thought. He covered his mouth reflexively, futilely.

They were charred bodies, darkened by flame, and covered in ash from end to blackened end. These immolated corpses were the source of the smell- that same smell from his dream.

Four, six, and countless more came shambling toward him as the winds around him picked up even more momentum.

Retching and gagging, Jonah backed away from the crawling corpses and tripped over the brick that was used to prop the door open. He fell hard on his back, and it knocked the wind out of him. Flat on the ground now, Jonah could see that the closest of the approaching creatures was now inches away from him. He rolled around, trying not to throw up.

It was a horrid sight, and Jonah closed his eyes tightly and turned his head away as he covered his face with both arms in some primitive form of defense.

Then there was an immediate silence that came so abruptly that it frightened him.

When he opened his eyes again, the sky was still, but the thick clouds of ash and dust remained blanketed over the atmosphere. The charred bodies and the acrid smell were gone. The sounds they made were gone, too, and he could hear nothing now save his own labored breath.

CHAPTER 5

C arlos placed the last crate of supplies onto the shuttle in the loading bay of the Factory. Finished for the day, he headed for the break room to gather his things and clock out.

The Factory's hallways were abnormally narrow, and Carlos brushed shoulders with more than a few of his fellow employees walking in the opposite direction. When contact was made, no one ever took it as a sign of disrespect or aggression. There was no avoiding it, especially for the larger men like Carlos, and there was nothing to do except reflexively grunt or apologize.

Every room in the Factory had a sterilized smell to it, like alcohol pads in a hospital room. Carlos could never get used to that smell or the memories it inevitably dredged up.

His footsteps made a soft, pattering rhythm that lightly echoed off the concrete walls. There were no windows, and the corridors were drowned in fluorescent lights that made blurred reflections on the tiled floors as employees shuffled past. Carlos walked with his head down, looking at his own beneath him. The mirrored image was an inverted man that opposed him with each step he took.

A young woman approached him from behind, lightly tapping him on the shoulder. He jumped, startled at the unexpected contact, and whirled around.

She was a good friend of his, a silent object of guilty desires that he consistently swore never to act on (failing only a few times here and there). They flirted occasionally, and he thought about her more often than any husband ever should. But their bond was closer than just workplace flirtations.

"Hey, Carlos. Do you have a second?" she asked.

"Sure thing, Cassie. What is it?"

Cassandra, or Cassie for short, happened to be the very same young woman that had been at the Jovial Fill-Up just a few days prior. Her face, which usually glowed, was cloudy and pale today—a stark contrast to the woman that Jonah had seen.

"I'm in a rough place, Carlos. A really, really rough place. I-" She put her hands over her mouth as if stifling a cry. "I'm... my sister is really sick. I'm really worried about her and..." Cassandra trailed off weakly as her eyes welled with tears. They streamed down her cheeks, forming clean lines down her face and pooled in charcoal patches on her dark-gray jumpsuit.

"Oh my god, Cassie, I'm- I'm so sorry. What happened?" he said.

"Well, you know how my brother... went a few years ago, right?" She spoke between soft gasps, trying her best to keep her composure. Cassandra put one of her trembling hands on Carlos' shoulder to keep herself still.

"Yeah, I do." Carlos remembered it all too well. Her kid brother, a husky boy named Seth, had suffered what locals called *the plague*. It had all happened so fast. The bright form of his youth swiftly transformed into the pallid frame of death. The disease started as just general fatigue, but it soon accelerated into hair loss. Then came the blood. Blood was in his stool, his vomit. He'd cough it up every day. Constant nosebleeds and throbbing headaches troubled him. He was littered in sores and always bleeding until the blood stopped.

Carlos remembered how heartbroken Cassandra had been throughout her brother's short fight. He also remembered how long it had taken her to recover after Seth died. This disease was not uncommon by any means in Gray Hills, and the local clinician, Dr. Gloria Harding, had documented several accounts of it dating as far back as fifteen years ago. (Although no one had ever seen these records).

But this made the prospect of dealing with it that much harder. Dozens of people had died of the very same symptoms, especially the young and old, but despite the doctor's best attempts, the cause could not be identified.

"Do you think that's what your sister might be," he cleared his throat, "going through?"

"Yes... it's just like—" but her voice broke, the levee of her remaining strength now crumbling beneath the force of her grief. Cassandra began to cry and repeatedly shook her head—a defiant *no* to the cruelty that had decided to darken her life a second time.

Carlos watched helplessly as she trembled and buried her face into his shoulder.

He, himself, had lost a son eight years ago—or was it nine? A boy who had only lived to be three before the same ailment took him. Oliver was probably too young to remember and, if he did remember, he never spoke about it. Maggie didn't either.

The Factory worker put his large arms around her

slender body, holding her tight as she cried with her face nestled into his chest. Carlos couldn't say anything that would help her, so he just held her until there were no tears left for her to cry.

After she had finished, she looked up at him with her eyes red and puffy and cheeks still moist with tears. She smiled at him, a bittersweet smile that signified more than any words or gesture could define. Cassandra sniffled, and Carlos offered the handkerchief he kept in his back pocket. She wiped her nose and face with it, then placed it into the pocket of her uniform.

"Thank you, Carlos. I mean it." She rubbed her eyes with the sleeve of her uniform and added, "You know, if you ever need to cry, I'll hold you in my arms too. To pay you back, obviously." Her voice was nasally, and she feigned a fragile smile.

"You'll be the first to know," he said.

Carlos put his arms on Cassie's shoulders and looked directly into her bloodshot eyes. She was in the process of trying to recompose herself, a feat in and of itself.

"Cass… you're better than this. I know your sister is too. Don't give up. You're stronger than you know," said Carlos, now patting her shoulder with his hand.

"*Sure.*" She sniffled, rubbed the back of her hand past her stuffy nose. "Whatever you say, Carlos."

"No, really. I mean, god, you're the strongest woman I know. The strongest *person* I know. Shit—I'd be lucky to have half of what you have. That…" he searched for the word, "*reservoir* of strength. Not many could live through what you have and still get up every morning."

She pulled him in quickly and kissed him. Her breath was hot and sweet and exactly like he had imagined so many times before. Just like the last kiss they shared. He kissed back, not feeling a pang of guilt in the moment. No, guilt lives outside of the moment, and it would come later. Not too much later, mind you.

#

The break room was a small and confined rectangle filled with a square table, a refrigerator, and posters that were put up as various forms of encouragement. One, the largest poster that the others seemed to constellate around, showed a large man in the dark-gray uniform of the Factory. His face hidden, features obscured beneath the shade of his hard hat, and his arms were raised in the air. In large, scarlet letters, it read *We Toil for the Greater Good of Humanity.*

Carlos scoffed at this.

He typed his name into a small terminal on the wall of the room, took his punch-out receipt, and stepped back out into the narrow hall.

Maybe I'll go check up on Jonah, he thought. He seemed pretty rough last night. And the night before that too. And the... well, he's just seemed like this for a while now. Carlos made his way to the parking lot, fished out his keyring from the pocket of his overalls, and unlocked his truck.

As he drove down the main street, he struck up a match and lit his non-filtered Factory cigarette. He inhaled, deep and slow, and felt his mind clear for a moment. As he exhaled, he noticed bits of the tobacco in his mouth.

The parking lot of the Jovial Fill-Up was barren. Carlos parked and stepped out into the dusk, armed with a box cutter that he'd grabbed from his glove box. He was on edge, terrified, but wasn't sure why he felt like there might be danger. It was an instinct, a matter of intuition.

He walked through the parking lot, between two of

the gas pumps, and slowly pressed his face into the large window of the gas station.

It was dark and looked empty.

He went through the automatic doors, manually pulling them apart. It wasn't locked, but the power was off. Everything seemed to be in its correct place. Drinks still stocked, canned foods on the shelves. There was no blood on the floor, although he had expected there to be. Why had he expected that?

He did smell something, though. The vague scent of roasting meat, a scent that reminded him of a dream he had a few nights before. One that head had not told anyone about.

There was still no sign of Jonah—no sign of anyone, in fact—so he crossed the store and slipped quietly behind the counter.

Carlos's work boots softly squeaked as he went, causing him to wince with each step. He flipped on the light of the supply room—nothing. He looked into the break room, but it was empty too.

The backdoor was open, lightly swinging and making contact with a small brick placed to prop it open. Carlos moved forward, trying to focus all the finesse contained in his vast body to not make a sound as he gripped the box cutter tightly in the pocket of his uniform.

Cautiously, he pushed open the door and stepped into the back lot.

There was nothing there.

Nothing save for the dumpster, a few pieces of trash that hadn't made it into the dumpster, and the brick that was placed to keep the door open. Feeling foolish at his cowardice, he turned back around.

He walked back into the station, bolder than before, but abruptly stopped when he saw a figure standing in the supply room. They had their back turned, dressed in a black coat, and their head was down. Once again, Carlos put his hand into his pocket as the person slowly turned around.

It was Janet. She quickly walked toward him, eyes wide with fear, and her voice was shaky.

"Oh, Carlos, thank god it's you. Have you seen Jonah? I came in for my shift, but the whole store was empty. I have no idea where he's gone. Do you know? His car isn't here." She sputtered the words, leaving little room for a reply. Carlos just shook his head.

Janet sighed deeply, placing her right hand on her head as if it was in pain.

"I can help you find him, though if you'd like." Carlos said. "I actually came here because I was worried about him after his odd behavior at the movies last night."

"Odd behavior?" she echoed, although it wasn't so much a question as just a vocal affirmation. "Do you know what happened last night? He... wouldn't tell me anything," she said, knowing that she had lied but not knowing *why* she had chosen to lie.

Was she ashamed that she had just walked away? But Jonah was the one acting like a lunatic. Who could blame her for walking away?

"Well, we've got to find him. Let me close down the store, so nobody tries to loot the place." She hesitated for a moment. "You'll come with me, right?"

"Of course," Carlos replied.

Gathering her bag, she stepped outside and locked the door as Carlos followed.

"Can we take your truck? I don't feel comfortable driving right now. I'm too... distracted."

"Sure thing, but do you have any idea where Jonah might be? Or where we could start looking for him?" he asked.

She shrugged. "No, not necessarily. We could go by

Jonah's place, but I doubt he'd be there." She paused, biting her lip. A habit of hers when she was deep in thought. "Our best bet would probably be to drive around in hopes that we can see his car. Then go from there. I mean, it's a small town," she said.

"It's as good a plan as any."

They loaded into his truck and drove off into the waning light of the evening. Their headlights shone brightly as they slowly moved through the various streets and neighborhoods closest to the Jovial Fill-Up. Then to Jonah's house, which was locked and had no car parked out front.

Then beyond.

CHAPTER 6

Jonah drove northwest in his rust-colored compact car. The sky hadn't changed; it remained the same putrid tint that he had seen earlier that day. It seemed to be a vision of impending destruction parallel to that of his dream. He wondered whether the dream had been a divination of the impending destruction of Gray Hills. Or maybe it was symbolic for his own destrcution. Possibly both.

The complicated thing about dreams is figuring out whether the underlying meaning is literal or figurative. Or nonexistent.

Were these signs a warning and was his dream a vision—a prophecy—of what was on the horizon? *If so*, he thought, *why me?* That was the question many saviors and prophets asked themselves, but they rarely did they ever receive any kind of answer that could be credited to a higher power.

Jonah, on the other hand, was not a prophet. He felt like a vapid gas station clerk hiding from shadows and yelling back at voices that hadn't spoken in the first place.

It was night now, already bitterly cold, and the sky looked like an inky black screen under the cover of night. There were no stars, only the moon, faintly shining as though it were a massive glimmering stone covered in a thick blanket of fog.

Jonah's hands were trembling as he drove toward the only place he could think to go. He hoped to find out who, or what, Farris was. This clue was all he had to go on, the only thing that kept him from surrendering to his feared lunacy.

One headlight—the left one because his right was busted—illuminated a worn sign for Elm Street. There were a few houses there, but most of them were vacant and damaged.

He drove past the street and, not more than a half-mile down, found another sign. A dark, wooden post, thick with what appeared to be dirt, leaning as if it had been struck by a moving vehicle. The bottom stood loosely in the ground and looked as though the slightest displacement of air would knock it down.

Jonah stepped out of the car, and with the sleeve of his jacket, wiped clean the words of the sign: High Street. He turned his head down what was once the road leading down High street but saw nothing but wreckage and dirt.

The same gray dirt that filled the sky, he thought. There were no buildings, just fragments; broken, splintered husks of what once was. He left the car and, grabbing his bag and a flashlight, started down the street.

The gray dirt—or rather, the ash—emitted a crunching sound with each step he took. An opaque murk of dust hovered around Jonah's feet like clouds threatening rain as he moved toward the ruins. He walked up a set of stairs; broken concrete shifted with his weight into the skeleton of a house.

He carefully stepped across to the half-wall, afraid that he may fall through the floor, and pointed his flashlight on a picture frame still hanging from what remained. Once again, he used the sleeve of his jacket to wipe away the thick layer of ash.

The picture showed a large gathering of people, something akin to a family reunion, and he counted twenty-three heads. They were dressed in green uniforms with blotchy, pixilated patterns of brown, tan, and gray. He didn't recognize their garb, although he felt like he should have.

None of the faces looked familiar, either. It was perplexing that he was unable to recognize even one of the almost two dozen faces. There were less than five hundred people in the entirety of Gray Hills; even if you didn't know a name, you at least recognized a face.

He took the picture out of the frame, placed it in his backpack, and stepped through the gaping hole where the door once was. He shone his flashlight on the ground and saw a small plaque that glimmered in response: *1307*.

And so he continued toward the other derelict structures, counting the numbers in his head on the odd side of the street until he arrived at what should be 1433.

The space looked as broken as all the rest—maybe even more so. There were no remaining foundations, no steps, or partial walls—just rubble.

Jonah walked around the perimeter, moving his flashlight as if it were a prison searchlight sweeping across the ground. When he got to what was once the back of the house, he stopped to cast daylight on a small concrete mound with a wooden door.

There was a cellar.

He reached for the rusted metal handle and, with one quick motion, swung it open. The door creaked from countless years of relative disuse and sharply hit a stone from the fallen edifice. It smelled of dry-rotted wood, an earthy scent that reminded him of the gardens of the Factory.

It was dark beyond the threshold, but not pitch black. A candle or weak light was illuminating the far corner of the cellar. He was terrified, but what else could he do? Turn around and act like the sky looked the same?

He pressed on.

CHAPTER 7

Margaret Stultus sat at her kitchen table, puffing on a Factory cigarette with exaggerated decorum. The ash grew and formed a long crooked line that hung over the ashtray, casting a shadow within her own. She flicked it and circumspectly put it to her quivering lips as if it were a loaded gun.

She drew in a slow breath, feeling the nicotine as it rose from her lungs to her head in a wave of guilty release. She looked at her hand and could swear she saw it shaking.

Then, she thought that maybe it wasn't her hand that was shaking but everything around it. It was an odd and frankly maddening sensation that she had felt only two times before.

One time, a few years ago—the exact number eluded her—she watched her son dying in his bed, cruelly splayed out on floral sheets of brightly colored marigolds. He coughed and cried and bled and coughed some more. There were sores under his arms, near his groin, and in his throat. They would burst, and he would shriek in agony. Then more blood would come.

It was amazing how much blood a human body contained, even in a person as small as her young son: only four years old, more or less, yet so much blood. Her pain at his passing was an immense and endless chasm of despair. All mothers who faced the loss of their child felt the same.

This did not bring Margaret any solace, though. Carlos wasn't there to give her any, either. Once they had known it was bad, that their little boy was leaving, his eyes grew vacant, and he left the house to drink himself senseless.

Rumors came to her a few days later, that he had gotten piss drunk that night and slept with a young Factory worker who met him at the bar, though he had decried any such notion as hearsay. She couldn't remember the name of the supposed girl, but she was long dead now. Plague. A pity, despite the rift the infidelity had caused in their marriage. She hated it when women blamed other women for their husband's poor decisions, as though the womb portended fault.

But she knew it wasn't her fault; it was his fault. It was Carlos' selfish desperation for any distraction from the truth that was waiting for him at home.

He had left them alone. Margaret, with one son dying and one still toddling, still hadn't forgiven him for it a decade later.

It was only a few minutes after her son drew his last breath that she saw it. Or rather felt it. Her hand was still grasping his face down on the bed, dirtied by sweat, blood, and urine. His hand had already gone cold.

How could it grow cold so quickly? It couldn't have been more than what, one or two minutes? But she could feel the warmth as it fled his little body like a smoky plume of breath in the cold night air.

Any remaining heat was merely reflective now, like stones in the desert after the sun had fallen.

In this thought or one much like it, she felt a shifting of the room like an optical illusion, a change in her visual field, a shaking. It felt as though she was shaking, but it looked as though everything else was. *That was ludicrous,* she thought. *How could that be?*

The second time was soon after her child's death. Relatively soon, anyway. Grief does funny things to memory, after all. It was under two years after, she was sure.

At Dr. Harding's office downtown, she had been waiting for Oliver to finish his check-up with the doctor. Sitting there in an uncomfortable chair, wanting a cigarette, she remembered hearing a woman next to her speaking to a friend.

The woman was talking about a young man, a cute little boy, who had died from the plague the previous month. She hadn't known who started calling it that. Plague—as though this was some town from the Dark Ages.

It always bothered her when they said that. Or maybe it bothered her because, deep down, that was the only word she could think of to describe it appropriately. An affliction that terrible had to be a plague of some sort, right? And so many young and old fell prey to it, year after year.

Yet, when people talked about it, they were so careless. They spoke as if it wasn't a terrible, impassive thing that marred the rest of your days: a cruel and indiscriminate scourge—an agent of chaos appointed by the universe itself.

Worst of all, some would forget those that had died from it. Like the woman before her right now, talking about a child. Struggling for its name and coming up short. The child had been her sister's kid, her nephew.

And she couldn't remember the name.

"It's been a fucking week," Margaret said, voice venomous in the quiet of the clinic.

"What?" the woman asked meekly.

"I said, it's been a fucking week since the boy died. That boy had a name. Can you remember it?"

The woman sat there, quiet and shocked by Margaret's words. Her mouth was open, flashing lightly yellowed teeth in the glaring light.

"Can you remember the boy's name?" asked Margaret again. This time with an emphasis on each syllable.

"… No," said the woman.

"His name was Jack!" She was yelling now, standing over the woman in the lobby of the clinic. "He was your goddamn nephew, Susan, and you can't remember his *goddamn* name."

It was there, standing above the wide-eyed woman and burning up with anger, that she had felt it another time. A slight shifting of everything around her.

This time, there was someone with her. Had Susan felt it too?

She would never know because she wouldn't ask her. How could she after a display like that?

Margaret was alone and looked alone in the darkness of her house with a single bulb hanging over her head. It emitted a small, dim spotlight on and around the kitchen table.

Carlos had not come home yet and was hours later than he had ever been without calling first. At least not since his drinking binge and possible infidelity ten years ago.

Oliver was gone as well, but he had been showing up late these past few weeks. He was a teenager, and thus a spirit that inherently moved in and out of moments as he pleased. A poltergeist of youthful rebellion, often absent, but sometimes capable of contact. It hurt for her to loosen the reins, but she didn't want her only—her remaining—son to resent her.

Mrs. Stultus snubbed out the butt of her cigarette and took a drink of Factory whiskey from the rocks glass in front of her. It burned her tongue and took her breath away as she swallowed. The burn maintained and traveled from her throat to her stomach and mingled painfully with the acid. It was rotgut and felt, at that moment, as though it were actually deteriorating her from the inside, dissolving whatever remained in her husk of a body.

The years have not been kind, she thought. She coughed, and the liquor inside her churned painfully.

The phone rang, a shrieking series of trills that made her jump in her seat. It rang once, twice, three times. She was fearful of what may be on the end of the line, knowing that her fear was without cause. Margaret shook herself back to her senses and answered the phone call on the fifth ring.

"Hello?"

A pause at the other end. There was light breathing and, just before Margaret decided to hang up, a voice replied:

"Hi... um, is-is Carlos... there? Carlos Stultus?"

The voice sounded stifled and a little nasally, as if the person on the other side had been crying recently.

Margaret was caught off-guard by the question. Her stomach burned, and the alcohol rose in her throat. She felt as though she were going to throw up. Is that why the bastard's late? Has he been fucking some younger girl behind my back? Goddammit.

"No, he's not here. May I ask who's calling?" Mrs. Stultus' voice was calm but brisk.

"Cassandra um- Cassie. Tell Carlos, Cassie called. I um... work with him. I just wanted to-to-to thank him for…" she hesitated, "talking to me. He's a great guy, you know? You're lucky."

Lucky? Margaret thought that luck had no part to play in whatever relationship her husband had with this woman. Vaguely, she recalled meeting her a few times at the factory and had exchanged a stray pleasantry or two with her at the supermarket. It was a small town, after all.

But there was an inkling that she had, a tone in the voice of Cassandra, that made her suspect something more familiar between her husband and the woman. Infidelity? She would have chalked it up to her insecurity had she not been drunk.

Margaret wanted to yell at her, to throw the phone across the room and scream obscenities with all the force her voice would allow. She also wanted to cry, to break down and sob for hours until she couldn't any longer.

But she did none of these things.

Instead, she let out a long breath that she had been holding in for far too long and simply replied, "Thanks. I'll tell Carlos you called." She hesitated for a moment and then burst out with, "Is there anything I should know about? Between the two of you?"

Margaret had intended for her voice to sound calm and even, but it ended up sounding strained, like a mandolin wound far too tight.

"No," replied the voice on the phone weakly, and the dial tone clicked on.

"Hello? Hello? Goddammit." Margaret shook her head and set the phone down on the receiver. A sharp exhale left her lips through gritted teeth.

The woman froze and tilted her head curiously. There was a noise outside, a low pattering that sounded like footsteps outside the front door.

She rose, grabbed her coat, then sat back down. She poured herself another drink and committed herself to ignoring everything else for the rest of the evening.

Then she heard three sharp raps on the door. Margaret rose with her coat still in her hands and put it on. She slowly walked to the entryway and peered through the eyehole with caution.

Nothing but stark black night.

The woman flipped on the porch light and looked out again. This time, she saw the railing, the edge of the driveway to her left, and various items that were strewn about the porch. But there was no life to be seen. No movement.

She unlatched the deadbolt of the door and anxiously stepped out. Only then did Margaret realize she was barefoot, as the ice-cold concrete of the doorstep made almost painful contact with her bare skin.

"Is there anybody out there? Ollie? Carlos?" Her heart was beating fast, and she could taste the combination of alcohol and stomach acid as it tried to rise back up for the second time tonight.

There was no reply. She repeated their names two and then three times. Still, nothing answered back except for the dull echo of her voice in the night.

Margaret went back inside the house, latched the deadbolt once again, and placed her coat over the back of the chair.

Closing her eyes, she felt as though her head was spinning like the wheel of a tilted carousel. Opening them again, she felt like she might throw up.

Margaret walked back into the kitchen and stared at the table. Her glass, which she had could have sworn she left upright, was upturned, and the liquid was gone—not spilled, just gone.

She lit a cigarette and stared at the empty glass on the table. "I'm drunk," she said.

CHAPTER 8

Jonah took a deep, shuddering breath and started down the wooden stairs of the cellar. He stepped as softly as he could, but the boards still creaked and moaned like ghosts calling to him from the other side. 'Go back,' he thought one said.

The cellar was dark and dank. It was a massive room with a dirt floor and moisture-laden brick walls. The smell was thick with dust and mildew. A few roaches scurried across the walls and earth as he waved his flashlight to scan the room.

A large door adjacent from the stairs—dry rotted—was the source of the faint light.

There was noise coming from behind the door, a rustling of pages. Jonah gasped softly. He reached for the handle, heedful of the danger that may lurk behind it but resolute in his search for answers. Yet he hesitated, and his hand lingered there just a few inches away.

What's waiting for me behind this door?

Before his hands could work up the courage to

touch the handle, the door swung open.

Standing there, a considerably tall man stood to face him with his back irradiated from the glow of a candle placed on a table behind him. Stacks of books littered the table, and some looked worse than the ruins above. The man had short auburn hair and tattered clothes.

He looked at Jonah, face stern but lean, sizing him up. His face was patchy with some sort of skin disease and sections of light skin intermingled with his almost ebony skin tone.

"What's in your backpack?" asked the large man with a calm voice.

"N-n-n-nothing. Just a b-book an-and…"

"Let me see what's inside."

Jonah was awash in the fear that overflowed within him. He felt outrageously stupid for not having a weapon with which to defend himself. Why should he trust this man who left his address with an attendant of a movie theatre?

He hadn't really thought this through at all. The man could be a thug, a murderer, a lunatic.

Obliging the stranger, he took out the poster he had received at the movie theatre, the picture he had found in the ruins of a house above, and finally the book. Something odd flashed across the tall man's face when he caught sight of the book.

"That book…"

"*All Things are Nothing,*" Jonah said.

"What?"

"*A-all Things are Nothing.* That's the name of the book."

At this, the man just nodded and stared at the book in Jonah's possession, recognition scrawled across his face.

"That book… I figured it had found its way here. I

was hoping it would have gotten here sooner, along with its true owner… but you're here. That means you got my message? I knew someone would, eventually."

"Wait… what? What do you… I um…"

"Good. We can talk about it here. You can sit down and tell me everything," said the large man.

"But… Who's Farris? I'm looking… for him. For Farris," sputtered Jonah as he followed the man into the room.

Once his eyes adjusted to the lowlight of the small room, he saw that it was partially furnished. There was a cupboard, a briefcase, and some other odds-and-ends. But there were more books than anything else. He'd never seen so many books outside of the small library in town.

"You've found him. I'm Farris."

"So then… what now?" said Jonah. He felt confused and scared. He was here. Now what?

Farris took the book and flipped to a passage toward the middle.

```
Everything is Nothing P. 72-73


     A  man  is  a  simple  creature.  A
disgusting  creature,  a  collection  of
fluids,  cells,  bacteria,  and  ill-
conceived  intentions  that  blend  into
the  beings  before  each  of  us.  The
being  that  is  each  of  us.
     All  things,  even  when  examined
with  the  weakest  of  attentions,  are
absurdly  pointless.  Life  itself,
therefore,  is  absurdly  meaningless.
There's  no  light  at  the  end  of  the
tunnel  or  a  bearded  father  judging  us
in  the  sky;  no,  it's  just  us.  A
product  of  the  mire  further  proved  by
```

our near annihilation just recently. We are petty and quick to anger, selfish, and foolish in equal parts. That will never change.

We all know this, deep down. Freud's Thanatos was stronger and more prevalent than he could ever have imagined. Our death drive knows what we have avoided our entire lives; we don't deserve to live. We shouldn't live. We use, we hurt, and we destroy indiscriminately. If not directly, then certainly by indirect means, which in some ways can be worse.

I am aware as I'm sure you all are. Everything in life, all life itself, ends as quickly as it seems to have begun when you consider the magnitude and longevity of the forever static universe. Such is life, and such is pointlessness. We are nothing. All things are nothing. You know what you have to do. Let me arm you, my friend, and may your end be a revolution against a familiar foe.

Farris flipped through the pages, reading slowly until his eyes looked to the light in the corner of the room. "This passage," he said, pointing to the middle of page 72, "is one that I have heard far more than I ever cared to. The man who wrote this, would you like to hear a story about him? About me?"

"...excuse me? A story? But I came here for-"

"-actually, it's better if I show you," said Farris as he returned the book to Jonah. Turning around, he pulled out an old reel and projector hidden behind the dust-laden pile of books beneath the table. He held it out to Jonah as if it were some relic of dire importance.

"Is that..."

"The film? Yes, *Bitter Wine*. It's a record of my last encounter with the man who wrote *that* book." He pointed emphatically at the book in Jonah's hand. "Ten years ago, now. Give or take."

Farris smiled slightly but there was no joy in it. It seemed forced, inhuman almost. He set down the projector and flipped on the switch of the machine. The projector whirred with a rattling and mechanical tapping as the film started.

It displayed a gray screen on a nearby wall, with oscillating waves distorting and dancing around the edges of the projected light. Then, an image gradually came into focus that showed a barren landscape, with some shacks surrounding a larger building that looked to have once been a gas station. There was a man amid the other residents of the town, taller than the rest. A man who looked very much like Farris.

The footage was grainy, and all of the sounds seemed distant as if they were coming from deep inside a well.

The film was displayed in black and white and appeared to have been shot with some old movie camera piloted by an amateur. *It was as if,* Jonah thought, *some old B film from the 1950s had been conjured into being, and the stoic figure next to him captured within.*

The scene shook, moving up and down but drawing closer to the man in view — the man in the room.

Farris moved across the room, away from the light, and sat silently against the far concrete wall. Jonah did the same and watched with the small hope that this would answer more questions than it would raise. He was wrong, of course. He was used to that, though.

Motes of dust fluttered and danced in the light of the projector like stars waxing and waning. Jonah watched them as they twirled about, and he swayed where he sat. The gas station clerk could feel his heart beating hard and his face felt numb with fear and apprehension.

What should I expect?

"There's some sound, but I'll fill in the blanks. There's more to the story than what you can see," Farris said. "But, that's always the case with these things. Stories, I mean. They're never as one-dimensional as they seem."

CHAPTER 9

The ground shifted beneath Farris as he walked through the gravel streets of a small town with no formal or remembered name. The whole place was worn down; dilapidated buildings and shacks littered the landscape, and what could scarcely be described as people were standing outside in the town square. Most of the men and women were in their forties or older, and their skin was discolored and deformed—a product of their environment.

Radiation poisoning was rampant, and despite the town being far from any past nuclear blast, the adverse effects still lingered like the shadow of a looming beast.

The sky itself was a sickly mixture of brown and black with dark clouds circling overhead, like the poorly painted landscape of a child god. The air was frigid and challenging to breathe, as could be inferred by the many coughs intermittently expelled by the crowd. The toll the mishap had taken on both the land and the people was still evident a decade later.

Farris passed several of the shacks and paused at one that had a rusted slide and deflated ball before it. He tilted his head to one side, curiously taking in the sight in front of him. There weren't any children to be seen or heard anywhere. There hadn't been for a long time.

Twelve of every twenty kids died from the radiation, the air quality, or cold. There hadn't been a child born in fifteen years; the parents couldn't bear to dig any more graves, so the beds of what few couples remained lay cold and loveless. It was a pain that those around him experienced far too often.

The disease, called by several names, swept through lives like a plague through a city. Bulbous sores covered the body, racking their victims with intolerable pain. They coughed and shit blood until there was nothing left of them—just an empty shell of what was once human.

He progressed through the crowd in what passed for the town square, gently pushing some more oblivious people to the side with his massive arms, like a man parting a coughing and belching sea. One he moved aside, a sickly older man, spat at him and shouted with the ferocity of a rabid animal that had been robbed of its territory. Spit bubbled and shot out as he bared his mangled, yellowed teeth.

"Get the hell outta here! You aren't going to change their minds. We'll be getting what we deserve soon enough," grated the man with contempt. Farris ignored his remarks and continued forward undeterred. He'd gotten used to this sort of thing.

"We'll be gettin' what we deserve, we'll be gettin' what we deserve, we'll be…"

He continued until the man's voice was a distant echo.

Farris stood before the largest structure in the town; a stone and metal building that had once been a gas station. The first part of the sign had been lost to the conditions, but the word *Way* could vaguely be discerned.

Windows were shattered and boarded up, and whole sections of the wall were missing. Two Gamut-7 model androids were standing on either side of the once automatic doors, now boarded up and augmented with makeshift wooden handles. They looked cautiously at Farris as he approached.

"Back again?" said the one on the left with a hint of concern in his voice. "We appreciate your dedication to the cause, but I don't think they can be convinced..." the android trailed off as Farris lifted his hand.

"Probably not. It's true. But..." He hesitated for a moment to regain his composure. "But I couldn't live with myself if I didn't try."

Both androids nodded as they grabbed the handles of the doors and opened them simultaneously. The movement was slow and emitted a grating creak.

"Good luck," whispered the one on the right as Farris strode passed. He nodded in reply and fixed his gaze ahead.

Huddled around an old wooden-door-turned-table were three people, speaking at great length about the 'issue'. Farris's feet rang through the empty halls, like church bells in a plague town. The people paid him no mind and carried on as if he wasn't there.

Mason Snare, the oldest of The Three, stood stone-faced as he listened intently. His face had deep lines and brown splotches that intermingled with his patchy gray beard. He looked at the one speaking, Esmee Child, who was only about half his age. She was as beautiful as anyone could be in this town; the hair on her head was long gone, but her skin was relatively clear.

Her eyes were a beautiful, intense hazel, yet her words were as menacing as the older man outside had been.

"Well, I think we should do it with wine. We've got what we need to do it tonight. The strychnine is in the safe, and we'll easily have enough for the whole town. This can end—tonight. No more deaths after this. No more suffering. God, we've waited so long for this. *I've* waited so long for this." Each subsequent word she spoke was increasingly emphatic and monosyllabic, to further drive home the importance of her point.

Esmee had once had a family; A mother. An aunt. Two sisters, one brother. A daughter and a son. They had all died within five years of one another, except for the boy named Carson.

"No, no, the strychnine is far too simple. No one wants that. We don't... we don't deserve it," replied Mason with indignance. He had lost his daughter to the disease two years ago and had never recovered.

There was silence as they processed what had been said. They stared at each other intently, waiting for the other to blink.

The third was a man named Albert Sterner, who had cold eyes and dark, greasy hair that clung to his forehead. He broke the silence as he adjusted the round glasses placed on the bridge of his nose. He kept his hand there as he spoke with a vaguely detached but calm tone, like a research scientist speaking to lab rats.

"We don't deserve *anything*. But Esmee is right. Strychnine is the only thing that can work quickly enough for the whole town. And... it's bitter." Albert smiled slightly as the last word left his crooked mouth. "That's something. Not a bittersweet end. Just a bitter one."

Albert had strode into town over a year ago, literally preaching on a milk crate in front of the square. He was received warmly with open arms from the beginning and had stayed there ever since. It had taken him less than two months to become part of the Three—

the previous Third had fallen down a cliff on a salvaging trip (may he rest in peace).

His words were nihilistic, defeatist ramblings. Yet, the people in that town listened to them. Life was pointless to them, and he only cemented that fact, armed them with the language of their anguish. Of their collective loss.

"Well, it appears I'm outnumbered," began Mason. "I guess—"

"No." Farris, who at this point was shaking with rage, walked up to the empty spot at the table. "This is no way to solve the problems you have," he pleaded rapidly. "You've got to stop listening to this… this—this charlatan!"

Sterner stared ahead, unflinching as he ignored the insults directed at him. "Now, now. There's no need for hostility. You've known this was coming. It's been planned for weeks. Just accept it. They have." His words were soothing, falsely so. He motioned to Mason, then Esmee, then out the doors and to the town in a parabola of hand gestures.

"It's long past any discussion. We've been over this with you several times before," answered Mason with a harsh croak. "We know you care for us. For all of us. But this *has* to happen. We can't bring kids into a world like this. We can't push forward. The Mother will recover without us. Faster without us here. Albert has the answers in his book if you want to reread it…" but Farris shook his head vigorously, violently.

In Esmee's rough, bandaged hands, she held a black and weather-ravaged book called *All Things Are Nothing*. It was Sterner's, a book he claimed to have written some time ago, and everyone in the town had read it many times over, from cover to cover. To those who couldn't read, well, he would gladly read it to them —every day, like Sunday service.

"I don't care what the damn book says… you can't do this. Things will get better with time; they'll improve. They'll…" He broke off as they motioned him away. Esmee tenderly placed her hand on Farris's shoulder and smiled up at him in a faint, condescending way, as if he were a child who couldn't possibly understand. Her hand traveled up his neck, slowly, and landed on a spot under his hair. There was a soft click.

She touched his neck, and he could no longer speak. His mouth vainly moved through a handful of syllables before he realized he wasn't producing any sound.

"Thank you for your concern, Farris. Really. But you can't stop this, and you'll be better off without us. Without me." The Three nodded in unison, and Farris sunk his head low as he turned toward the door, dejected.

He wandered past the two androids who now looked at him with silent sympathy. He could tell they wanted to say something, but couldn't. It wouldn't have helped, anyway. After all, wasn't it the empty rhetoric that had led them all to this point, a town dangling from the edge of a cliff? Ready to fall, and happy to do so?

Farris pushed back through the crowd, slower this time. They were still speaking and coughing, but he couldn't make out any of the words that were said. He only knew that there were more than a few curses directed at him. Yet, most of them stood excited, staring at an empty, makeshift stage with rapt anticipation. Waiting for what was about to come and welcoming it, once again with open arms.

He moved past the houses and rusted toys, past the eyes that watched him as he walked away, all the way to the edge of the town. A hill overlooking a valley on the far end of the village was his destination.

The valley was dark and ominous as it spread out

below him like a vast canyon. There were small bits of gnarled metal and ash littered upon the ground, and the earth itself was gray and barren.

He wanted to jump in, but he knew he couldn't. It was against his imperative. Besides, what purpose would that serve?

The sky, still brown and black with dirt and soot, darkened as the faint sun fell. It looked like a black hole, ready to swallow the entire town.

Farris turned around slowly and saw the two androids from before standing behind him. They smiled at him. It was a pitiful attempt at consolation, but he was thankful for it, nonetheless.

"You did all you could, brother. There's nothing else," one said with hushed sobriety. The other nodded, still intent on keeping silent. Farris, an android himself, could not speak. Esmee had made sure of that when she deactivated his vocal relay. He didn't want to turn it back on.

What good had words done him? Empty rhetoric, hollow ideals that culminated into nothing. No, not nothing. Culminated into the death of an entire town. Not his words, but words nonetheless.

Instead, he outstretched his hands to both of them. They each grabbed one of his arms with one of their own as they looked out onto the town. The three androids bowed their heads as if in prayer.

In a certain sense, they were praying, sending their will to whatever power had more control over the world than they did. Knowing that these inward words, this outward projection of theirs, would likely fall on deaf ears. *Just like all other prayers*, thought Farris.

#

It was dark, but small shining columns exuded from

flashlights and torches in the town square. The crowd grew louder, a low-rumbling wave of sound, and he could vaguely make out The Three standing in front of the impatient gathering.

They watched the lights for a while and listened as the crowd began to settle down once again. Barely intelligible, Farris heard the people say in one proclaiming toast, "May we get what we deserve."

As the leaders held up the book, each of The Three placed one hand on its black binding as their other clutched a glass. The crowd held up their drinks as well and repeated the words with a haunting, coalescence of sound.

Farris felt a pit in his stomach, a knotted pain that confounded him.

Why had he even tried to stop them?

Esmee.

She wasn't like the others, at least not until Albert had shown up. She was always so determined, so full of life until that *man* came and ruined it all. It was Farris's job, his imperative, to protect the town and the people within.

They had been programmed to do so.

The androids were recovered wreckage from the old world, re-purposed for this small, ash-covered town. They were to be their guardians. Protectors.

And, for him, he wanted to protect her most of all.

"May we get what we deserve."

Each of them drank, except for one.

It had only been a few days ago that Farris had sat next to Esmee at that very same spot. Looking out at the town, talking, and enjoying what little contentment could be gleaned from this harsh life. But now...

Farris watched as every light went out, one at a time in swift succession, like candles being snuffed out. Then there was silence—an eerie silence that filled the soul with dread and kept the body from moving, even if that body wasn't flesh.

The three androids buried them the next morning at first light.

CHAPTER 10

Farris rose to shut off the film and looked at Jonah expectantly, face solemn. The gas station clerk sat there, clutching his knees tightly. His eyes were wide, and he could feel his heart beating with the fervor of a hummingbird.

"I'm sure you have some questions," said Farris.

Jonah blinked as if not quite comprehending the words. He felt dazed, and his head hurt.

Once comprehension finally did find him, he slowly nodded in affirmation. "Who was holding the camera?" asked Jonah.

"That wouldn't be my first question if I were you." Farris laughed, but it sounded hollow. "It wasn't a person holding the camera. It was a surveillance drone. They're mostly gone now, but there used to be more. It had... begun following me around, I think. For what reason, I can't tell you."

"What happened to it?"

"To this one or them as a whole?" asked the

android.

"Both," Jonah said softly.

"I took apart this one and stole the footage it had recorded, so I could... show others what happened. It was my duty to protect the town, and I had failed. So, me and my brothers- the other androids- we dedicated the rest of our lives to protect what remains of this ramshackle world." Jonah felt as though there was also some sentimentality for Farris keeping the footage, but wisely kept his mouth closed.

"As for them as a whole, they were sent from the lunar colony a couple of decades ago—a year or two after the fallout and the subsequent migration—to keep an eye on the remaining settlements. Most of the settlements are gone now."

"I've never seen a drone in Gray Hills," said Jonah.

"Don't worry about that. There isn't one here. It's not necessary."

"Not necessary?"

"Never mind. Forget I mentioned it," but Jonah didn't want to forget anything anymore. This appeared to be a vital piece of information that Farris was purposefully withholding. Why not tell him everything? What use could it serve to hold back now? Jonah chose not to press the matter but suspected that there were limits to how much he should trust the android before him.

"So… this Albert Sterner is the author of-"

"Yes," replied Farris briskly.

"And who is he in all of this? I mean, why did he do that? And why'd he leave the book?" Jonah shook his head, bemused. The android kept his back turned, putting the projector back where he had gotten it. "Did he leave the book?"

"Albert is an enigma. He does what he wants for reasons all his own. He doesn't like to get his hands dirty. He may have left the book or he may have had someone else leave it on his behalf. It's hard telling. But, what we can be sure of, is that Albert wanted you to find it."

"But why me?"

"That charlatan probably thinks he can use you for whatever game he's playing at."

"Like when he made..." Jonah struggled awkwardly for a moment, trying to choose his words carefully. "Like what happened in your town," he amended.

"Exactly like that. He strolled in, unbeknownst to everyone, and played the people like they were expendable pieces on a board. *Human lives.* My town wasn't the only time this has happened."

"Why do you say that?" asked Jonah.

Farris turned away.

"Wait here a moment." The android ruffled through one of the various stacks of books scattered around. After a couple of minutes of rummaging, he located a worn piece of paper carefully placed between the pages of a thick book. He held it out to Jonah, who looked at it with a scrutinizing eye.

It was a map, with several areas marked throughout with blue circles. Some of the rings were crossed through with two thickly scrawled diagonal lines, forming a red X.

"What is this?"

"A list of the towns that we know of- *knew of.* Most of them are gone now."

"You think he did this to all of them?"

"No... not all of them. Disease from heavy radiation and harsh weather in areas that don't receive sunlight do damage to those with weakened immune systems. There're also roving bands of maniacs just killing and taking what they want. Believing that this is their world now. But, a few of the towns we've investigated held some clues that might point to him."

"What kind of clues?" asked Jonah.

"What you'd expect. There's a man in a sackcloth robe carrying a book. Sometimes they claim it's a different title, though, and not all of them are… dealt with in the same way." Farris' face grew contorted, and he looked away. "Yes, it was Albert who left that book." He looked down at the floor, eyes narrowed. "But I'm done with answering your questions for now. Why don't you answer one of mine?"

"O-okay."

"What led you to me?"

"A poster with an address on it," said Jonah.

Farris looked at the man intensely. "I'm aware of that. I'm the one who left the address, remember? Or are you just suffering from another symptom of your town's collective misremembrance?" said the android contemptuously to the man in front of him. He started to walk out of the room. "Maybe this was a mistake."

"No! I'm… I'm sorry. I'll explain it all to you. Please, don't make me leave. I-I need to know what's going on."

The android bowed his head in condescending acquiescence.

Jonah described in great detail all the events that had led him to a dark cellar on a nonexistent street in a world that was no longer his own. Farris listened intently but showed no sign of emotion or reaction until he was finished.

They had now moved out of the cramped room and into the adjoining area. Farris paced around as Jonah continued.

"So… am I just out of my mind? I… what about the sky? The book? The rock? The figure? The-the beetle-thing that chased me in the movie theatre parking lot!?"

"One thing at a time. The creature you saw, I'm not sure what that was. But I believe it has something to do with Sterner. He knows something about this town that I don't. This settlement's different than the others. It was set up by the colony, whereas the rest were just groups of people that survived the mishap. I think that the rock and book are a message. He's messing with you, taunting you. Calling you out."

"But why?" asked Jonah in a voice higher than he'd have liked.

Farris sighed and looked away.

Jonah watched him curiously, wondering whether there were any wires that he could see. He had a sudden urge to ask details of what real androids consisted of. Jonah had seen *The Creation of the Humanoids* a couple of times at the Neon but felt pretty sure that real androids were different.

Jonah knew that this wasn't the time or place for such questions, so he bit his tongue.

Yet, he also found himself wondering how an android could be destroyed. Was it as easy as killing a human? Were they just as fragile? Just a well-placed shot from a gun, perhaps. Or were they virtually indestructible? Jonah felt fear at this last part. He wanted to trust Farris but couldn't shake the feeling that at least two separate forces were manipulating him. Maybe even more.

Perhaps one of them is the machine with you right now.

"I honestly don't know why. I don't know why that monster does what he does, as I said before. But I intend to end it. Now, the sky..." Farris hesitated, knowing that what came next would not be easy for the confused gas station clerk. "I don't know what you and everyone else in this town can see, but the sky, the way you describe it to me, is how it really is, just like you saw in the film.

81

Your town isn't immune to what happened. No place on earth is. *They've* done something to you, altered what you and the rest of Gray Hills can see." He gestured with both hands above his head.

"Who's they?"

Farris looked annoyed but let it go. "Those up above, on the moon. But, never mind that now. Like I said before, one thing at a time."

"Those on the moon? On the colony?"

"Yes," he said sharply, "and I estimate that the altered perceptions of the residents of Gray Hills are an attempt to make you all more..." He grasped for an appropriate word. "Complicit."

"Complicit, how?"

The android shrugged. "To make resources for them, I would guess. To keep you all blissfully ignorant down here, toiling in a world that is rampant with radiation and dust. Perhaps other reasons, too."

"Okay, but if you don't know the answers, then where do we find them?" Jonah himself had begun pacing in a circle, trying to understand the impossibility of everything said. No matter which way he calculated, it just didn't add up.

"We find the charlatan. And remember, Jonah, no matter what *they* did, Albert is the one we need to find. Our only concern right now."

"I… guess that makes sense," said Jonah weakly but he wasn't sure he agreed.

He couldn't help thinking of the colonists. They were supposed to be the ones struggling, and Gray Hills was supposed to... but it was all a lie. It had to be. He stopped his pacing and clenched his fists. *If I get the chance*, he thought. *After Albert, I'll make them tell me why. Somehow.*

Farris didn't like the gas station clerk, but he was useful for now. Bait to keep his enemy distracted.

The android had grown bitter over the years since the incidents of *Bitter Wine*. Harder. He had never been able to catch up to the man in sackcloth in all his years of searching. He had gone to settlement after settlement, but he was always too late.

Esmee. His thoughts often turned to her and, when they did, he felt all the sadness that he was able to. Scientists had once called it artificial emotion. Yet, his feelings didn't feel like an emulation of something real. They themselves felt real. So long ago, he had argued with his creators about who he was.

But now, he was here. That world was long gone.

Farris finally knew where to find the man who had caused all his sufferings. How could he just let that moment slip through his fingers like water through a poorly weaved basket? He had felt the pain deeply, the pain that absence left, and it fed a fulminating hatred that replaced what used to be there. This overrode all other thoughts for him.

And he had a plan.

He was hopeful when the man came into the cellar, introducing himself and stating his business. Farris had been hoping someone would come. He couldn't quite explain how someone might be drawn to the film and try searching him out. It was just a hunch, based on past experiences with the game that Albert played.

"Will you come with me? I know he'll be expecting you sometime soon. He seems focused on you," for some reason, thought Farris. "Maybe if we leave now, we can catch him by surprise."

Jonah seemed decent enough if a little dim. Farris had shown him the film and explained the parts that couldn't be seen — left out the parts that weren't necessary. Yet, the man seemed not to understand the gravity of it all. He had been beset by taunt after taunt by Albert but still found the gall to be asking stupid questions.

The android was courteous enough to feign kindness for the time being, but it wasn't easy for him.

At least, Farris thought, *I don't really like him. He probably won't make it through the night.*

Yes, he needed to use the gas station clerk to further his ends. He would still do it even if he did like the man, mind you. But, not liking Jonah meant he'd be free of some of the forthcoming guilt.

Would that guilt be emulated, or real?

"Are you ready?"

"Yes," said Jonah, knowing he had no other choice at this moment.

"Try to keep up." The android led him up the stairs, out of the cellar, and into the gray world beyond.

CHAPTER 11

C arlos and Janet drove through the empty streets of Gray Hills, searching for Jonah's eyesore of a car. The headlights of Carlos's truck cut through the night, slowly illuminating the dark corners of the town. He lit his cigarette in his right hand as his left tightly gripped the wheel. Janet's golden hair flowed in the breeze of the open window as the smell of cigarette smoke lightly assailed her senses.

She had never liked the smell of cigarette smoke, but for a brief instant considered asking Carlos for one. Yet, she knew that she'd end up regretting it; first, she'd retch at the earthy taste of the tobacco, then she'd feel lightheaded and dizzy from the rush of nicotine, and then she'd just be even more upset than she was now. If that was even possible.

"Seen anything yet?" Carlos puffed his cigarette; eyes fixed on the road as he spoke. Janet had been covering her face since she had gotten into the truck.

"No."

She rubbed her temples carefully with the palms of her hands. A migraine was coming on, and she was having trouble focusing. *Yeah, nicotine definitely wouldn't help,* she thought.

Janet was worried about Jonah. Fear for her friend gripped her chest like a vice. They had checked his home, looked through closets and even upturned his mattress. All she had found there were a small collection of notebooks filled with sloppily scrawled lines of poetry.

It wasn't bad poetry, though, from what she could make out. Janet didn't know much of things like that, as poetry wasn't common in Gray Hills. She hadn't expected that out of him. For Jonah to be good at something caught her off guard and made her feel even worse.

They canvased the neighborhood surrounding his house, wandering around the small block and asking the neighbors who were home if they had seen anything. They had all replied negatively.

"Where the hell could he be?" she muttered.

Janet, you have no idea what I've been going through. He had said that to her, and she had ignored his plea for help. That's what it was, a plea. *He was out of his mind, and you,* she thought to herself, *told him to stop and stormed off. Some friend you are.*

You have no idea what I've been going through. Those words continually rang through her head from the moment she arrived at the barren parking lot of the Jovial Fill-Up. Those words, and the anguish carved on his face that last time she saw him.

The two were silent. The only sound that broke the silence was the gentle rhythm of the engine and the rush of wind coming through the open windows.

The rest of the town was quiet too.

"I'm sure everything's fine." Carlos wanted to be

reassuring, but his tone was unconvincing.

Perhaps aware of his transparency, he looked at her, taking his eyes off the road for a moment and letting periphery guide his way through the empty streets.

"You... I'm worried too. I um... I should've talked with him, should've seen this coming. I did, honestly. I just..." He gestured, turned back to the road beyond the windshield, and continued, "I didn't want to accept it as a *real* problem. But, to be frank, there've been red flags everywhere. I had dinner with him the night before the movie, and he kept shifting his eyes around like he was scared out of his mind. Then he— you saw how he was at the Neon. Breathing hard and covered in sweat after he had left for some fucking reason. It's just I've known him for so long and..." Carlos trailed off, eyes wet.

He felt very tired all of a sudden. Janet gently touched his shoulder, rousing him from his thoughts.

"It's not your fault. We'll find him." *It's my fault,* she thought.

It wasn't long after that when the headlights of Carlos's truck illuminated a lone car pulled off to the side of the street. The two approached slowly, cautiously.

The headlights revealed Jonah's car with its bright gaze, sitting alone in the empty wasteland beyond the town. Carlos had half-expected to see his friend dead behind the wheel, mouth and eyes open, riddled with the terror that confronts us all in our last moments.

His heart sank at the thought, and he suddenly wanted to be home with his wife and son, playing cards or eating dinner. He wondered what Maggie and Ollie were doing right then. They were likely asleep. Carlos craved the warmth of his bed but stared instead at the emptiness of his friend's car.

Then he thought of Cassie. Maybe he could go to her house tonight. He could think of some passable excuse to tell his wife. He had done so before.

Maggie and he had been drifting apart for a while now. He loved her, yes, but a man has needs. He had needs. And his wife, once warm and loving, had been as cold as the night for far too long now.

Guilt filled him. Guilt for thinking the way that he did and guilt for thinking it now of all times. When his friend was missing. Possibly dead.

Janet turned to him, blinking. "What... where is he? Why do you think he'd leave his car here, in the middle of nowhere?" Her voice was subdued, but her hands were shaking. *Was it fear for her friend or fear for herself?* Carlos wondered.

"I... don't know. Let's take a look around." He turned away from the empty car, now looking at her. Footprints led west from where they stood, down the remains of what was once a street. Carlos couldn't see a sign, and he had never been this far out of town.

Seeing how bothered Janet was, he added, "I can go, and you can stay here if you want. I can handle this by myself. I'm a strong guy, no matter what the girls at the Factory say," he joked but neither of them laughed.

He was a man who had trouble expressing himself and would often turn to humor to cover up how he felt about a situation. The loss of his son, the death of a sister. A missing friend who may be dead too. They were just too much for him, and deep down, he felt weak.

She shook her head. "No, I want to go with you." He was relieved at this. Carlos was scared too, although he'd hate to admit it. And Janet, she was a strong woman. Stronger than him.

Cassie, he thought, *what I'd give for her to hold me now. To smell the sweet perfume of her presence and to feel my head tightly pressed onto the softness of her chest, wrapped in her embrace.*

Yet, another voice spoke in his mind. It was similar

to his own but deeper and slightly distorted. *But, what about Maggie, and your son goddammit!? Are you that cruel? Some people would jump for joy at the love that you have, at a family that reciprocates that very same love. Yet, you scorn your wife and child and you string along that poor woman, too. Despicable.*

The back of his head throbbed, and he fought tears that burned and rose beneath his eyes. Carlos shook his head, confused, and the voice suddenly stopped. He had never heard voices before and, if it wasn't for the façade of courage he had already raised, he would have likely broken down then and there.

But he couldn't help but wonder; *What did it mean? Why now, of all times?*

They both got out of the truck, metal doors clanging in the stillness of the night and echoing throughout the string of decaying houses ahead of them.

The two didn't look back to see the flickering lights of those still awake or unable to sleep in Gray Hills. A strong wind swept passed them, tousling the dirt around them. It didn't bother them. They each moved forward with bated breath and somber hearts.

CHAPTER 12

To *Carson,*

It's been a long time since we've been able to talk. I haven't really had much time, given everything going on. Obviously, aside from the whole world going to hell in a handbasket thing. I've thought a lot about what I should do, and I've come to a decision. It's not one that I can make lightly.

I'm going to try to stay here and make do with what I know. Besides, I could never get enough money to make the trip with you. All my life savings, everything I've got left, I will use to get one of my children to the moon. You're the only one I have left. The only one I can save.

Please know that I wish I could go with you. It's okay if you hate me after this. I won't blame you. But know that I did this for you. To ensure your survival, no matter what. It's a mother's duty, after all.

I'm going to miss you. I'll be going to a small

town, a squatter's camp more than likely, but it'll be someplace with other people. I can't be alone now. Not after you're gone. Please, be safe and stay with your guardian. She'll keep watch over you in my place.

With all the love,
Your mother

CHAPTER 13

The two men stood on a broken street that had once been a hub of pedestrians and cars. It now lay tattered with large diagonal slabs of stone haphazardly jutting from the ground like obelisks from some long-forgotten civilization.

Jonah held out his hand and touched one as he walked passed.

The stone was sharp and coarse, like those found in the aftermath of a fire-bombed city. The word Dresden came to his mind, but he couldn't explain what that word meant or where it had come from.

It was as though, Jonah thought, *an earthquake had shifted the entire earth around them.*

It was difficult knowing what had been natural and what had been caused by people. Or by a giant, dust-covered machine created by humankind. By this point in time, they may have both been working the means to the very same end.

There it stood, a grand and monolithic cathedral

that persisted untouched among the surrounding rubble. They were only a dozen-or-so miles outside of Gray Hills, but this world seemed so much different than the town that Jonah had known all his life.

It seemed closer to the town in *Bitter Wine*. Farris's town.

Is this how it really was? Had the event that caused the supposed great migration been like that climactic scene from the Time Machine, leaving people displaced, injured and crushed by falling debris?

Jonah wanted to call it all a lie and go back home. Back to his life. But how could he? Some of what the android told him was surely a lie, but not this. It was laid out before him, a sordid reminder of a past he couldn't remember or properly know.

He shook his head, tried to calm the thoughts that filled his addled mind. This was the world that he and the people of Gray Hills had been left with, this broken place that had been unwillingly thrust upon them.

Why couldn't he see it before? His life, before tonight, had seemed like a mist as thick as the ash that concealed the stars in the sky. If he was honest, he wasn't sure of anything anymore.

Just one step at a time. Here and now, he inwardly told himself.

The moon shone behind the tattered buildings, but it was a faint light that provided little guidance through the steep streets.

Farris led the way, confident that this was where Albert Sterner had been. *But how?*

"How do you know he's there?" Jonah asked.

"I just know," replied the android harshly.

"That's *not* an answer." He had matched Farris's harsh tone and impressed even himself when the words left his lips.

The android heaved a sigh. "It's not. You're right.

But I can't give you a proper answer. I'm... drawn to him. Like magnets. Opposing forces being pulled together, but not quite like that. I haven't the words to explain it to you. Not right now."

"Do you think he'll know how to explain it to me?" asked Jonah after a moment of silence.

"Who? Albert?" Farris lowered his head. "Maybe. But, even if he does tell you the answer to this question or the countless others you have, they may be lies. Or half-truths."

And in what way are you two different?

They walked to the rear entrance of the church to a door with a curtained glass window and a blue handicapped sticker that pointed to a ramp. The door had once been sealed by a welded metal bar, but the seal had recently been broken.

They entered slowly and found themselves on a landing with two sets of stairs. One went down into what was likely to be a storage area or bsement. The other stairs ascended into another hallway that led to the sanctuary and a slew of other miscellaneous rooms. The walls were covered in cream-colored wallpaper, and the ceiling stained with dark blotches of black mold.

The two climbed the stairs, feet softly brushing on the mildewed carpet. They were in a wide hallway with no no windows. It was dark and difficult to see more than a few paces ahead.

"I'm going to take a look downstairs," said Farris. "Don't wander off." Jonah listened absently as the android's steps receded.

He walked up to a wall where a picture was hung, adorned with flakes of paint and torn strips of wallpaper that made its awkward placement look even more disheveled.

It was a portrait of a man whom Jonah did not recognize, donning a crown of thorns. He appeared to be shirtless, pale-skinned and drenched in sweat and blood. Jonah felt some pity for him.

The man in the portrait did look familiar, though. Something to do with his childhood and the songs sang so long ago.

Across from the portrait, there was an ornately furnished table covered with a moth-eaten tablecloth. There were candles situated on both sides of a large leather-bound book. Jonah approached the book, flipping through the pages until he arrived at one passage that caught his eye.

Revelations 6:12: *And I beheld when he had opened the sixth seal, and, lo, there was a great earthquake; and the sun became black as sackcloth of hair, and the moon became as blood.*

"Aren't those the words that the black figure had whispered to me a few nights ago?" he said quietly to himself. But what did they mean? Then, and now?

There were a series of soft thuds behind him as Farris lumbered back up the stairs.

"There's a way to the sanctuary down there. An old stairwell in a storage room. You go through those doors and talk to him." He pointed past Jonah to a pair of ornate wooden doors. "Get your answers. I'll take care of him from behind. You keep him distracted," said Farris as he began to walk away.

The android stopped, seeming to ruminate on something. "Don't mess it up."

"Will I be okay?" asked Jonah softly.

The android kept his back to Jonah. "Of course."

Farris went back down the stairs, walking as quietly as he could, and Jonah swung open the large, heavy doors leading to the sanctuary.

There were two lines of pews on both sides of a great strip of gold carpet that led to an altar that was carpeted in the same fashion. The surrounding carpet was a drab and pale green, which further accentuated the bright color in the center.

Moonlight cascaded through the stained-glass windows in rows on both sides of the sanctuary made the altar seem to radiate. There was a wooden pulpit placed on the altar, and a large lower-case "t" was hanging on the wall behind it. The whole place smelled of burnt matches and lightly scented candles.

Halfway down the aisle, standing directly between the two sets of pews was a man. Although the sanctuary was dimly lit, Jonah could see who it was that stood before him. He had seen him on film, in black and white, but he looked the same standing ahead of them. Older now, perhaps. Or was it just a trick of the light?

There had been several signs, each subsequently leading him and culminating to the point he was at now.

The man he knew as Albert Sterner smiled wide.

Carlos and Janet walked through the abandoned neighborhood surrounding Jonah's deserted car. The night was coal-black, and they were both on edge. The sky, which had been very clear earlier that evening, had grown thick with an impenetrable cover that Carlos could never remember seeing before. There were no stars, and the moon had lost its luster.

There was such a complete and utter lack of sound, so much so that he could hear the pulsing rhythm of blood pumping through his ears. He listened to the air whistle through his nose as it filled his lungs with breath and heard it again at the exhale.

The silence was so uncomfortable that he inwardly wished for some sound, any sound, to break the silence that pervaded everything around them.

"So... do you really think Jonah's okay?" asked Janet, it seemed to just hear herself speak, to fill that space. He didn't mind.

"I certainly hope so." Carlos turned and saw worry visible on Janet's face. "I'm sure he's fine," he amended, trying to be reassuring but failing to be. They had already been over this, but words were comforting. Or, at least the sound of them was.

"What if he's not?" she said.

"Well, then there's nothing we can do about it. But, as far as we know, he is okay, so there's no need to worry about worst-case scenarios. It'll just create unnecessary-" but Carlos's sentence was cut short by a deafening, sharp crack that rang less than a mile west from where they were walking. It boomed, seeming to shake the very world around them.

It was a gunshot.

They both ran back to Carlos's car, stumbling with anxious panic, and drove west as fast as his truck would take them. Neither wanted to speak anymore.

Slanted edges of what were once streets and sidewalks blocked their path, so they continued on foot.

They heard three more gunshots as they made their way to the source, running now. Fearing the worst.

CHAPTER 14

S o, I've been discovered, it seems." Albert's wide smile looked menacing in the faint moonlight. His crooked mouth bared sharp, triangular teeth, and he wore a frayed robe made of sackcloth dyed black.

Like the figure I saw outside the Jovial Fill-Up, thought Jonah.

"You know, I've been waiting for our palaver for days now. I'd left a trail for you. Clues. And you have followed them diligently as if Providence itself had led you," said Albert in a garish voice that rang through the sanctuary like church bells. The hood on his robe was down, revealing long, greasy black hair that hung like curtains on either side of his face.

He had aged since that time, a decade or so ago when he was in that town with Farris. When he had held up a cup, watching the others around him drink, and then set down that very same cup to admire his work.

Walking toward the altar, Albert stopped at the crest of the stairs. His feet were only seen on the rise and gave the appearance of hovering over the carpeted floor. Looking down, he cocked his head at the gas station clerk in a look of bemusement.

"I'll be blunt. How would you like to know the truth?" asked Albert.

Jonah met the man's gaze for a moment and then looked down. His mouth was dry, and his tongue felt like a wad of cotton.

"Come on, son. I know it's been gnawing at you. A hungry dog that's been nipping at your heels for a long time now."

"I-I-I do. I mean, it-it has been gnawing at me." Jonah was terrified and puzzled and angry all at once. He was gripped with fear as he strained to speak. Words did not come easily for him. Especially not now.

"Very well then, I'd be happy to enlighten you. I'm sure that an old machine has spun quite the yarn regarding our sordid past, but I aim to bring you up to speed concerning the matter. Here and now, as they say." He looked at Jonah slyly. *Here and now.*

"So, my dear Jonah, what questions do you have for me?"

Jonah blinked, licked his lips, and cleared his throat. He tried to speak, but no words came.

"Don't be shy," he said.

"Why isn't there a drone in Gray Hills?" asked Jonah, awkwardly spilling the words from his mouth like a cup overflowing with wine. Stupid question, but he spoke clearly, which surprised him. There were so many more important things he could have asked. Yet, this was better than nothing, and he couldn't stay silent. Not now. Jonah had asked the same question to Farris, but in truth, he felt that the android was holding something back, withholding some information or feelings. *Something.*

"And tell me the truth about the colony," he added.

It was an afterthought but an important question, nonetheless. The radio broadcasts, the factory that shipped supplies to them, what did it all mean? And why, if the world had been destroyed—relatively speaking—were there still people on the planet when there had been a migration? Why was Gray Hills unlike the other settlements in that they had continual contact with the moon? All of these were the questions rushing through the thick murk of his head, but his trembling lips only spoke two.

"Ah, both good questions. Though that second one isn't really a question. Well, anyway, this is going to require a bit of backstory. Is that all right, Jonah?" asked the man with what appeared to be real sincerity. Or a well-practiced simulation of it.

"Yes." His hands shook. He could see Farris in his periphery, slowly opening a door at the far corner of the altar. About two dozen feet away from the man in sackcloth. The android looked fixedly at Jonah, motioning for him to stay silent.

"You see, other settlements in our world are unable to contact the lunar colony. They are *anomalies*, other people who survived the mishap of a couple of decades ago. Many migrated to the moon, as you know, but some eked out an existence here. People are determined if nothing else.

"Now, once the migration was complete, they realized after only six months that they lacked the resources and the real estate to keep going. What could be produced in the colony was not enough to sustain the population, and gardening was hard on the infertile ground. There was barely enough space for the people living there and not enough food for even half of them. Quite a predicament, wouldn't you say?" asked Sterner.

He had a voice that made you want to listen. Even its soft echoes reverberated with the aftershocks of authority. Jonah nodded, enraptured by his words.

"So, my dear Jonah, they created a sole town that would provide additional resources to the colony. Supplementary to what the colony could produce. That town would be built around a large, multipurpose Factory. Thus, maintenance drones are used to keep tabs on those lawless settlements outside of the colony's control, to protect this lifeline, but Gray Hills doesn't need one because it is in constant contact already. Under constant control," he amended.

A shadow had passed over Jonah's face. "Okay, but why…" His head looked to the ground again. It felt heavy all of a sudden, over-encumbered by what he was hearing. *It was too much*, he thought. "So, you left the signs? That's what you said earlier."

"Yes. The book, anyway."

"But… what about the hallucinations? And my dream? Th-the sky is different now, like in my dream. It's like how it was in Farris's movie. All that about the —what did you call it—*mishap*. How come Gray Hills doesn't—or at least didn't—look like that before?"

"It's all the same answer: *The book*," he said, this time with more emphasis.

"I don't understand."

Farris took another step forward, a serrated blade shaking slightly in his hand as he began to close the gap. Jonah hadn't seen him pull it out, but the metal glinted softly in the nebulous light filtering through the windows.

"Well…"

"And you didn't answer my second question," said Jonah. This was bold, especially for him. Was it the fear, the almost palpable terror, that stunned his usual demeanor?

"What was the question again?" The man smiled, either with patronizing irony or as an attempt to emphasize his words. His sharp teeth seemed to glow in the low light, like pearls on the ocean floor.

Farris motioned for him to move forward, a slight flexing of his free hand, but the gas station clerk stayed where he was.

"The... what's actually going on with the colony? I-I know that—"

"Yes, an excellent question indeed," the man on the altar interrupted, clapping his hands in exclamation. "*The* question, in fact. I..."

"Just tell me!" Jonah wasn't sure if it was the anger of the prior interruption or just pure confusion that gave him the courage to speak like this. To a man who was capable of... what exactly? Many things, it seemed. And the tension of distracting such a man, while another tried to kill him, wasn't an easy task for him. He was not a naturally deceptive person and feared that any wrong move would give him away.

"Very well. Going back to the colony, you know how they needed one settlement to make resources? Well, my dear Jonah, they found that few were willing to put themselves at risk for fear of death by radiation. Well, those up above had an idea. You see, the greatest minds were among those that migrated—along with those who had the right amount of money—and they had been developing something called an Occipital Perception Transmuter. An OPT, we called it. It's this fantastic device that could be placed in the occipital lobe of a person and then, there it is! They would see the world in a whole new way. Forcibly so.

"Of course, altered perceptions were not enough, so they would wipe the memories of those implanted with the OPT beforehand. A simple enough task, truthfully, that I used to help with." Albert's voice lilted, songlike, with the timbre of a harp through those once hallowed halls.

"Used to help with? Is that how you know all of this?" asked Jonah.

"Well, I've wanted nothing but to be transparent with you." He cleared his throat, then continued, "I was an assistant of the scientist who spearheaded the OPT project. I was... more than that at one point. But that's another story, and I fear I wouldn't have the time to tell it.

"The way the OPT works is... complex, but I'll do my best to explain it to you. It's located in your brain, at the back of your skull," and he touched his own as he said this, gently tapping the back of his head, "near the primary visual cortex. Just slightly altering the signals coming in, those sensations of the world around you, a shade of gray can easily become blue if you know what areas of the brain to stimulate. It also has wires that spread like tendrils to your hypothalamus and pituitary gland, sending electrical impulses to force the inhibition of cortisol, which the body produces during stressful circumstances."

Farris had almost closed the gap. Jonah, however, still did not move. He stood there, mouth open, as he tried to absorb the implications of what was being said.

"Why!? Why all of this extra work?" he asked, practically yelling. Sweat trickled down his face despite the cold that pursued him everywhere he went. At that moment, it occurred to him *why* it was always cold in Gray Hills; the damaged atmosphere was too thick for sunlight to heat this ruined world.

"Well, to help keep you happy—content, at least—changing the color of the sky, making one see twinkling stars and a full, bright moon isn't enough. Have you forgotten about the plague?"

"What about it?" asked Jonah.

"It's no plague. It's an adverse effect of the radiation. From the *mishap*. That very same danger I mentioned before. You see, this planet is not safe to live on. But they need *you all* to live on it for the short time you can, so the colonists can live safely up there as long as possible." He pointed one thin finger at a stained-glass window where the moon could be seen glowing faintly in the thick haze of the sky.

"And all of these extra features are to keep you calm, sedated. It also sends those same impulses to the hippocampus and amygdala, the memory and fear centers of your brain, respectively. That's why, when people die or terrible things happen, you don't remember it. At least not vividly after the fact. How many times have you said the words 'I can't remember' when you so severely wished you could? Fears and emotions create vivid memories. Without fear or the stress response... well, I'm sure you get the point."

Jonah swallowed hard. "And so, when there's something that we should remember, something bad, it knows to send those impulses to... those parts of the brain? So we won't remember them as strongly?" He spoke in a flurry of words. Farris was too close now. There wasn't much time, and he was grasping at understanding it all. So many things seemed to be over his head.

Albert cocked an eyebrow. "Close enough. Thus, Gray Hills was created as a Factory town that shipped resources to the lunar colony. The inhabitants lived in forced, yet blissful ignorance of the true state of things. You find that people are much more complicit in their toil when it's under a blue sky. This is what Gray Hills has always been. So many have died, and so many more will. It's a dangerous place, you know. Even if you couldn't see it until now. And those hallucinations of yours? Just a simple malfunctioning of your OPT. An unfortunate side-effect of the deactivation process. Courtesy of..."

"The book," said Jonah quietly. "How?"

"There's a device in the book. A jammer that disrupts the impulses that direct your perceptions. It should have resulted in a simple degradation of false perceptions. Yet, it seems the results are not without," he paused, and gave a slight nod toward Jonah. "Side effects."

Jonah's mouth was open, gaping, fumbling with words, possibilities. Questions with no answers. "But why me? Why did it have to be me?" he asked.

Albert smiled. "You've been forcibly blinded. You can be more, and you deserve freedom. The autonomy to be what you want to be. *They* took that away from you. Not me—them." He pointed at the window once again.

"I knew you would be the one, the only one, who could do what was needed—if you so choose to. Call it a feeling. Or a whim. Truthfully, all I want is to free your town, Jonah. I've constructed a much larger signal jammer on the roof of this building. It should have already begun affecting some of the residents. I'm sure you're purpose is to stop me. To kill me. Or to watch me be killed. But don't you want them to be freed?"

"I don't know", murmured Jonah, almost unintelligible.

"Well that's all I want. Stay here and destroy the machine if you want. Freedom affords us the ability to make whatever choices we want. You can leave them to their ignorance. Some say there's some bliss in that. Or. *Or,* you could take the fight to the colony. You could demand answers, recompense, for the tainted lives you have all been forced to live."

There was silence.

Jonah didn't respond, but he did lower his hands from his eyes.

When had he covered them?

He could see the outline of Farris standing close to

Albert now—striking distance.

Arm raised, the blade glinted in the faint light of the moon, and on that glimmering blade he could just make out another moon. There was the one in the sky and the one on the blade. Perhaps there were more within further reflections, thousands of variations of the same place, the same event, the same people. All hurdling toward the same moment. Helpless in this.

Displaced by the events that had led him here, he could almost see the puppeteer above him, pulling the strings. When had his will left him? And, which of the three above was the true architect of his fate, the author of his listless life: Albert Sterner, the android, or the colony?

CHAPTER 15

L ook out behind you!" Jonah cried without even realizing it. One moment he saw Farris standing so close, and then the next, he heard his voice fill the surrounding space. The android froze for a moment, within arm's reach of Albert, and glared at the gas station clerk with a look of betrayal.

The man in sackcloth turned his gaze to Farris, and although the smile remained on his lips, it faded from his eyes. "Now, it's been far too long, hasn't it, old friend. Where do the years go?" Albert lifted both hands like the cups of a balancing scale. "Some here, and others there. Always an attempt at equilibrium. Just like with those before, eh? The residents of our little town?" He looked down, feigning sadness. "A real pity."

"You're a goddamn monster!" said Farris through gritted teeth. Albert exchanged his wry smile for a look of mock disbelief.

"Me? Heavens no, I'm no monster. No devil, daemon, or darkness incarnate. I am, as you must already know—" and he motioned to the android "—a *relay*. I merely pass information to those that are willing to listen. And then those who listen choose to act accordingly. But you, Farris, were never a very receptive sort. Ironic, eh? You block out the truth and avoid it like *it's poisonous*."

The last two words were spoken slowly, in an almost musical cadence, as if the man in sackcloth was a child teasingly remarking at a lost game.

"It makes no difference to me" he continued, "And, more importantly, no difference to the truth. It is and always will be quite objectively based, old friend."

"What do you know about truth?!" demanded the android. His voice was harsh but it didn't seem to carry authority in this place.

Slyly, Albert's hand slipped into the pocket of his robe. Jonah barely noticed it. Had Farris?

"Did you know that your friend over there knew all of this?" Sterner turned back to Jonah. "What we were discussing—or most of it, anyway. He knows my handiwork by now. He just wanted to use you as bait, Jonah, to get to me. He doesn't care about Gray Hills or you. This is all about revenge for him. Nothing more."

The android looked at Jonah and pleaded, "Don't listen to him. He's just trying to turn you against—"

"Come now, Jonah," Albert interrupted. "How else could he have gotten you here? He needed to leave questions unanswered. To make you think I was the only one who knew those answers."

Farris hesitated, looking at Jonah. "That's… a lie. He's trying to—" But before Farris could finish, the world was awash in a blinding light. A thunderous sound filled Jonah's ears, made even more so by the large space of the sanctuary.

The android had been shot in the side. He twirled around and took a few faltering steps forward. His mouth was open in surprise, and he raised the knife as if still hoping to complete what he came for. Before he made it another step, he was shot three more times; twice in the chest and once through the forehead.

That first shot was deafening. It rang through those once hallowed halls and cascaded into seemingly infinite echoes. Those echoes were soon replaced by a high-pitched squeal so loud Jonah couldn't even hear the next three shots, just the damage they left in their wake.

Farris tumbled down the steps of the altar, face down on the carpeted floor. Gray liquid pooled around him and glistened in the low light of the moon—a midnight lake before a golden shrine.

Albert stood on the altar, holding the gun he had pulled from his robe. Lowering his weapon, he walked toward the emergency exit out of the church. He turned back to Jonah, lingering at the threshold.

"I've talked, and you've listened enough for one day. Now you must *act*. I have acted as the relay and you as the receiver. Do what you believe you need to do. What you *know*, you must do."

"And what is that?" Jonah asked, pleadingly.

Albert Sterner smiled. What was once an unnerving smile seemed suddenly to settle Jonah's nerves.

"You have the information. Or, the information we have time for. Others are coming, I fear. Do whatever you want with the knowledge. You can follow me, kill me if you like. Destroy the signal jammer at the top of this ruined building. Or you can take the fight to them. Those who did this to you and the rest of your town." He shrugged and beamed a smile that seemed to diminish the gun in his hand and the act it had just committed. "The choice is yours."

Through the doors of the sanctuary, Carlos and Janet came running. Carlos ran past Jonah and down the aisle toward the emergency exit, and Janet fell to her knees, looking at the lifeless form of Farris on the ground. He seemed very human as he lay there.

Jonah looked back to the door, but the man in sackcloth was gone. He hadn't even heard the door creak or close.

Janet held the head of Farris between her two cupped hands as he was quietly trying to speak through a stuttering series of whirs and static.

"Get him. Get… Albert. He was—I'm sorry."

Janet's brow furrowed. She looked down at the android in somber bemusement. "What's going on?"

"Ask… Jonah." His body convulsed on the floor, and his eyes flickered. Then they darkened.

Carlos came running back, panting with his hands on his knees and his head bent down. He wiped away the sweat on his forehead.

"Bastard got away," he said between breaths. He looked down at Farris. "Who—or what—the hell was that thing? And where's Jonah?" When she looked around, Jonah was nowhere to be seen.

He had already run out of the sanctuary. The darkness and commotion had given him ample cover to go unnoticed, through the emergency exit and around to the front of the church.

Jonah couldn't talk to them now. *No*, he thought. *It wouldn't do any good*. It was just earlier that day, a lifetime ago now, it seemed, when he had tried to explain it to Janet. He remembered—all to well— how that had turned out.

The time for talking had passed, and Jonah needed, for once in his life, to take his life in his own hands.

Jonah ran as fast as he could, expertly maneuvering between massive slabs of stone that blocked the path to the clearing ahead. His head was throbbing, and his throat burned. Tears were welling in his eyes, making the world around him look distorted.

He ran to Carlos's truck, which still held the keys in the ignition. Turning it over, Jonah sped off toward the Factory.

CHAPTER 16

Dear Esmee,

I don't know how to begin this. I've hated you for so long. Night after sleepless night, I'd lay awake, staring out at the Earth. What was I looking for? You?

I don't really know.

I've been here on the colony for what must be almost ten years now. God, where does the time go? It's been hard here. So goddamn hard. You know, after all that money you spent to get me on the shuttle, I'm still only an Echelon-Five.

Echelon-Five, the bottom of the proverbial barrel.

Not that anyone can actually move up. At least I haven't heard of it.

I thought I'd die up here without you. But I've made do. I've scraped by with what work I can find, and, despite all the pain, I do hope I've made you proud. Not that you'll be able to know what I've done. I know there's no way this letter will reach you, but I've got to write it just the same. It's cathartic to say these things even though you'll never be able to reply.

You may be long dead by now.

I hope you're not, but I've heard the reports. The drones have sent footage of the world below—your world, now—and they've broadcasted it as a display of the savagery we've left behind. Ascended from, as they so tactfully put it. It's a useful tool whenever the approval ratings are down.

There are times when people complain about the colony and reminisce about what their old homes were like. Before the mishap, obviously. When that happens, the Echelon-One's broadcast video footage of bandits coming through and wiping an unkempt settlement off the map. They occasionally show videos of a tribe of cannibals in the area that used to be Dayton, Ohio, brutally preying on passersby.

Those are the worst ones.

You know, the scariest thing about that footage is that people don't seem to recognize it as real anymore. We watch up here, safely if underprivileged, as those left down below are torn apart again and again and again. And all we can think, all we honestly think, is, "I'm glad that's not me."

I'm glad that's not me.

Then again, some of us water at the mouth at the thought of gleaning some vicarious pleasure at the suffering of our long-lost brothers and sisters. At the splatter of blood across the ash-encrusted landscape or the ripping of ligaments by a group of people who look more like dogs than their primate ancestors. I've watched as that tribe in Dayton put a leg on a spit. I threw up shortly thereafter.

I'm sorry. I'm rambling the way I used to when I was a kid. Even in imagination, I regress to the child I was when talking to you. I said before that I've scraped by despite my low caste, but I've done more than that. I've thrived, as best I can. I have a wife. And a child on the way. I'm naming her Annette after my sister. I miss her, but I know that she's gone.

It's the not knowing about you that keeps me up at night.

By the way, in case you couldn't tell, I forgive you. I really do. It's easy to forgive the dead.

With all the love,
Your son Carson

CHAPTER 17

The landscape slowly shifted from the wastelands outside of the town to the blocks of houses and businesses that were the staple of the Gray Hills Jonah knew so well.

Had known.

That gloom above, the actual sky, cast the whole town in a trickling light that spilled ominously from the eastern horizon.

Jonah's hands trembled as they gripped the steering wheel so tight that it hurt. They hadn't stopped shaking, and he could still hear the ringing in his ears, like a shrieking cacophony of birdsong. Tears streamed down his face and blurred his vision.

He absently switched on the radio and listened to the tail-end of a colony broadcast.

...and that's it, folks. You heard it here from our good friend Bobby Branham, a Factory worker at our sister town of Gray Hills. He's one of those hardworking men and women who make sure that we can survive up

here. And, let's be honest, folks, he's probably got it better than most of us up here do. Down there in Gray Hills, there are blue skies during the days and clear nights filled with twinkling stars. There is freedom of movement and peace of mind. Safety, unlike here, is a guarantee for all those that toil away. For the greater good, I might add *laugh track*. Well, Bobby, I sure envy you, and if I weren't needed up here, I'd trade places with you in an instant. I mean, the sheer beauty of-

He switched it off.

The light of the sun seemed to crackle beyond the ash in the sky and looked like white noise on a television screen. Jonah drove by people, some of whom he used to know, and saw their smiling faces greeting one another. Some waved at him, but he stared past them.

He wondered whether any of them had dreamed of destruction last night. Whether any of them would hallucinate today. Freedom would come at a price.

Driving by the clinic, he saw a line of people waiting patiently for it to open. There were young and old, all coughing and spitting as they waited to be seen. In the frame of the ashy predawn light, Jonah thought he saw a young man that he recognized standing in the window of the clinic.

He kept driving.

These past few days, his life had felt like a piece of driftwood caught in a rapturous current, pulling him one way and then another. Never giving him any say in either the direction he was pulled or the destination that awaited him. He had been manipulated from the start, but that was going to change. He would take control of his own life, no matter the consequences.

And it all started with a plan.

Jonah's plan, as he understood it, was to sneak into the Factory with the keycard Carlos had left in the truck, hijack a shuttle that carried supplies to the moon, and head for the colony.

And then... what? Much passed that he wasn't sure. He was acting mostly on feeling rather than rationale, the judge instead of the god.

He parked the truck around the backside of the Factory, out of view from prying eyes, and made his way to the side entrance that some of the late-night employees used. He slid the keycard. It sparked green after a moment of anticipation, and the metal doors clicked and opened.

The hallways of the Factory were deserted; otherwise, he would have surely been caught. His clothes were tattered, and his hands and face stained with dirt, ash, and gray blood.

How had he only noticed now, looking at his distorted reflection in the glossy floor of the Factory, that some of the android's blood—or whatever it was— had gotten on his clothes and face?

After taking some wrong turns in the maze of the factory, he eventually arrived at the shuttle dock. He heard a rustling inside. One employee was on staff, likely there to keep watch. He felt the sweat as it trickled down his back. Took a breath and let it out. As slow as he could manage.

That employee happened to be Cassandra, but Jonah didn't immediately recognize her in the heart-pounding mania of the moment.

Slowly, he crept along the wall when her back was turned. She held a clipboard and was looking inside a wooden crate. The factory worker was checking to make sure the required goods were all accounted for in preparation for the shipment going out the next day.

First one foot, then the other. Inhale, exhale. One foot, then the other. Inhale, exhale.

He had made it halfway to the shuttle when he

heard her yell. "Hey! You're not supposed to be here!"

Jonah quickly glanced back, momentarily frozen like an animal in the hunter's sights, and then began to sprint as fast as he could toward the shuttle. Cassandra, like all the dockworkers of the Factory tasked with security, was armed with a taser gun in case this very situation was to occur. She yelled at him to stop again, but when he persisted, she dropped to one knee and aimed her gun at his back.

Calmly, she let out a breath and pulled the trigger as the black vines of the stun gun extended towards him like grasping hands.

Jonah quickly fumbled for the keycard in his pocket to open the door of the shuttle. He swiped it, praying that the dull bulb would flash green.

It had to, he thought. *It worked out there. It had to work here too. Please, god, let it work. Did Carlos have access to the shuttles?* He couldn't remember.

It changed color just before the barbs of the gun dug into his back, and he made it safely through the shuttle door that swung open. He closed it behind him but could hear the vines of the stun gun as they knocked on the door with a dull thump, like a stone striking a wall.

The gas station clerk looked around, unsure of what he should do next. The shuttle was filled with crates of supplies and blinking lights that seemed to swim around his vision in a sea of incoherence.

Jonah hurriedly sat at the chair in front of the control panel and flipped on the switch marked auto-pilot. Thankfully for him, all the shuttles had a navigation system that directed them to their only destination, the lunar colony.

Air began to rush beneath the craft with a sound like the blades of a helicopter as it built up speed before its ascent.

The ship jolted forward, shaking as if reluctant to

move, through the open area of the Factory roof as Cassandra dove to safety, presumably yelling stray curses directed at him.

The shuttle rapidly rose up through the thick clouds of ash and dust, rattling as Jonah gripped the arms of the chair. He saw the Factory and the Jovial Fill-Up, his house and the Stultus house, all shrink to the size of a child's playset.

The ship flew through the layers of the atmosphere, twisting and turning as it climbed higher and higher. He gasped as the force and speed of the shuttle's ascent knocked the wind out of him. It kept climbing for what Jonah thought might be forever until it finally broke through the exosphere, and he saw laid out before the blank canvas of his perception the boundless and infinite ocean of space.

And he had never seen anything so clear, real or imagined.

CHAPTER 18

Carlos was driving Janet to the Jovial Fill-Up in Jonah's beat-up car since his own had been stolen. At least Jonah, the bastard that he was, had been 'kind' enough to leave his keys in the ignition.

His initial thought had been to try to find Jonah, but he had quickly abandoned that notion. He still had no idea what had happened or what his friend was planning to do, but he didn't have the fight in him.

He felt tired and wanted to get some rest. *Surely the situation could wait,* he thought. Janet had initially protested but eventually gave in due to her exhaustion. It was no use killing themselves from sleep deprivation, they had decided.

Yet, and he didn't mention this part to Janet, Carlos just wanted to be done with Jonah and whatever madness he had gotten himself into. He had stolen his truck and, more importantly, put his life and the lives of his friends in danger. How in the hell could he forgive that?

Carlos dropped her off next to her car and waved his hand swiftly in parting. She forced a weak smile and returned the gesture.

As he drove back to his home, Carlos felt the exhaustion begin to overtake him and had trouble keeping himself awake. He cranked up the radio as a motivational song played. Crackling and whining, it spilled clumsily from the half-busted speakers in Jonah's car.

He pulled up to his house and saw his wife standing on the porch, arms crossed as she leaned over the railing. Margaret stood there, eyes glaring, and brows knitted. Carlos, who was initially overjoyed at the sight of his wife, was quickly made aware that the feeling was not mutual. Immaturely, he had thought about driving past the house, but he decided against it.

As he pulled into the driveway and got out of Jonah's car, Margaret turned to him with a series of different emotions passing over her face like the ever-shifting form of a Rorschach inkblot test. She opened her mouth once, then twice, but no sound escaped her lips.

"Hello," Carlos said as plainly as he could.

His nonchalance had gifted her the strength she needed. "Why are you driving Jonah's car? And where the hell is your truck?"

Carlos sighed. "It's a long story. I'll tell you after I get some rest." Carlos tried to go through the front door but was intercepted by his wife.

"Everything is a damned long story. I feel like there's a lot that you haven't been telling me. How many long stories do you have dancing around in that skull of yours?"

Stunned, he took a step back. Then, attempting to match her anger, he said, "What are you talking about? I've been out all night, searching for Jonah. I saw a man—or what I think was something like a man—get shot. Then Jonah ran off, as well as the shooter. He fucking stole my truck, and I don't know where he went, and I don't—"

"I don't give a fuck about the truck or Jonah right now, Carlos. What I want to know, what I *really* want to know is whether you've been seeing someone named *Cassie* behind my back." Carlos' dark skin grew a shade paler.

"Yeah, I talked to her," Maggie continued. "She actually called while you were out doing god knows what. She was asking for you." Fury flashed like lightning across her face.

Carlos sighed once again. He put his hands to his face and covered his eyes. The thought of attempting a lie occurred to him, but, tired as he was, he couldn't muster the strength to create one. Sidestepping the question, on the other hand, he could still manage.

"Listen, Maggie, Cassie is a co-worker. An employee of the Factory. And yes, I'd be lying if I didn't say there weren't some... sort of feelings between us. But *you* are my wife. Not her. Earlier today, she was vulnerable, and I was comforting her and..." Carlos trailed off because the phone started to ring from inside their house. Margaret waved her hand in dismissal, shaking her head, and passed through the threshold of their home. Carlos followed, in a mental whirlwind created by the events behind and before him.

Margaret stood with the receiver in her hand, gravely nodding and listening to some detached voice that Carlos could only hear as muffled sounds. She said, "Okay, so what does that mean?" and "What're we supposed to do now?" Fear and concern were apparent in her tone. "Okay, we'll be down there as soon as we can," she said as she hung up the phone.

With eyes unreadable, she looked at Carlos.

"What is it?" he asked, anger still unintentionally

creeping into his voice.

She now looked as though she were stifling tears. "It's Ollie, Carlos. He's at the clinic. He was on his way to a friend's house last night and passed out in the middle of the street. That's why he never came home." She shook her head, angry at herself for not going out to look for him. For getting drunk and forgetting all about him until the phone rang. "He's at the clinic now and-and, and they think he has…" She hesitated for a moment, not wanting to say it.

"Has what?"

"They, they think he has what our… what our other son had. What so many people here have. Carlos, they want us to get down there as quick as we can."

"Okay," he said and made his way back out the front door and started Jonah's car once again. She followed suit and closed the door behind her, a trailing apparition of a woman.

Despite their unfinished fight, their anger and mistrust, they held hands as they sped toward the clinic to see whatever it was that remained of their only living child.

He was tired, so goddamn tired, but the endorphins from the church still pumped through him, further augmented by the fear of what would happen next.

Carlos searched the early morning sky for any sign or indication of what was to come next, but none could be seen beyond the pale haze on the eastern horizon, and the dim glow of the moon. It was almost full but not quite, and Carlos couldn't tell whether it was waxing or waning.

Waning, he eventually resolved.

CHAPTER 19

The clinic in Gray Hills was eerily quiet in the early morning light, and despite it being past dawn, the horizon had not ransomed its daytime hue. The whole town was in a state of liminal existence, transitioning from the night before to whatever the current day would hold.

Carlos was still in his uniform, smudged aimlessly with ash and dirt, and he held an unlit cigarette between his shaking fingers. He absently stared off at some unknown point away from Margaret. She couldn't see his eyes, but she suspected his stare was a vacant one.

Margaret looked at her own trembling hands, and they seemed foreign to her. They had to be someone else's hands, surely. Could these blotchy, wrinkled fingers truly be her own? Where had the time—and her youth—gone? Wasted. Wasted on a coward of a man and children who left her alone in this empty and unforgiving town.

But that wasn't fair. It was never their choice to leave. It was the world around them, harsh and cold as it was, that continually beckoned them away from her. Stealing them when she needed them most.

She needed them all the time. They were her children and how dare anyone, anything, any cruel god or universe take them away from her. She wanted to scream until her voice broke, claw her fingers at the ground until they were bloody stumps. Margaret wanted everything to stop, to freeze how it was, so she could be suspended at this moment, never forced to live another. Perhaps her life was a case study in the resilience of life in the face of indiscriminate cruelty—the perpetually suffering wife and mother.

Margaret shook her head, fighting the tears that threatened to come even after so many had been shed. Her eyes narrowed, looking at the form of her husband, and she cursed herself for still feeling a dull warmth at his sight. It quickly passed, almost quick enough for her to ignore.

"Why?" she asked. He stood there, still, except for his hands, as if he hadn't heard a word. "Why?" said Margaret again, this time louder. On any other day, she would have inserted a bit of bite in her words, but the fight had long fled her husk of a body.

He turned around slowly, as if that small action took all the strength he could muster and fixed his eyes on her. Carlos looked like shit; eyes bloodshot and face stained with dirt—but seeing his face made something churn in her.

"Why what?" he asked with a voice that sounded distant. It was as if he was answering from the bottom of a pit.

"Why is this happening?"

He looked down, face impassive. "I... don't know."

"Does it even matter to you? Do you even care? I've been *here*. Every single day. With *our* son. *I* picked him up from school. *I* took him to the Neon to watch movies. I watched over him, talked to him, cherished him every day of his life. But you—you've been holed up in the Factory, doing god knows what with that. And now—" her voice choked as she failed to suppress a sob.

"I—"

She broke in. "No, Carlos. You don't get to speak. You lost that right the moment you decided to cheat on me. You've been spending more and more hours at work for what I thought was an attempt at making our lives more comfortable. I always thought that, yes, you were *there*, but you wanted to be *here*. With us. But that was really just an excuse for you to—"

"I never slept with her," the words blurted out in a garbled mess that seemed to surprise him.

She threw her hands up and gave a fake half-laugh. "Sleeping with her wouldn't be the worst thing you've done! You—forget it. This is what you do. Every time tragedy hits, you're out the door. Honestly, I bet you've had one foot out the door for years now. Ever since… *Goddammit*, I was the one who had to hold him when his left breath rattled out—our little boy. You left, said you couldn't handle it. You'll leave again."

"I remember it differently." His voice sounded like a whimper. Margaret couldn't even understand the words. It sounded so unlike him, that pillar he had once pretended to be.

"What?"

"I remember it differently," he said a little louder, enunciating each word.

"Of course you do. I think… *no*, I'm done."

He took a step toward her, eyes finally looking into her own, and she took a step back. "Maggie, you can't. I need you."

"Find solace somewhere else," she said and turned away from him. "Maybe you can call Cassie. But I don't want to see you. I don't want to talk to you. And honestly, I don't care if I ever see you again. This life has taken so much from me, but for all things I can't do without but have been forced to, I can do without you."

She walked away briskly, as fast as she could without running, and didn't dare to look back.

#

Margaret sat at her kitchen table once again, hands intertwined and steepled as though in prayer. Her head ached at the base of where her skull met the spine, and her vision was a thick fog formed from copious amounts of tears and whiskey.

She peered at the edge of her Factory cigarette, watched as the ember flared and dimmed with her breath. It was a tiny signal flare sent into the empty sky of her life.

Her face was a smear of eyeshadow and inebriation, sorrow and defeat. Hair messily tied up like a coarse nest of wire, streaks of gray mixed with the bits of auburn that she had once felt nostalgic for. She didn't feel much nostalgia anymore, though.

Wan of complexion and heart, drained of all that had once given her color. The only color, aside from that bit still left in her hair, was the dab of rouge on her cheeks and nose from the whiskey.

The room shook around her, twirled, and danced with a clumsy magnificence that she lost herself in. Drowning in a warbled stream of lights and colors and shapes that she couldn't make out, Margaret let them swallow her up; She didn't care if she ever woke.

It was that feeling, three times now. No, four. Yes, four times that she felt that shifting of the world around her. She basked in it, bathed in the dissolution of her surroundings until they were a pinprick so far away that she couldn't recall where she was anymore.

She woke up several hours later with the headache persisting even stronger than before, but the blissful ignorance of her prior inebriation had left her alone.

Almost alone.

On the table, near her splayed hands and empty rocks glass, she saw an old leather-bound book. *All Things are Nothing* was the title, displayed in a golden script.

How had it gotten there? She hadn't heard anyone enter the house. She must have been sleeping heavier than she thought.

The woman called out to her empty home in a voice still heavy with drunken sleep. "Is anyone there?" No answer. She bobbed her head, waiting for a reply. "Hello?"

She tried to stand up, felt the twisting knots of her stomach and the blurring of her periphery, and promptly sat back down. *If there was anyone in the house before*, she thought, *they're gone now*.

Margaret looked at the book for a moment, opened it to a dog-eared page, and began to read.

All Things are Nothing, P. 39
Our worlds come crumbling down around us in the blink of an eye. The world itself, wrought with hatred and strife, literally succumbed to the most significant loss our Mother has ever felt. We hate those bombs, those harbingers of destruction, but should we?

CHAPTER 20

J onah's head was still throbbing, and his throat
prickled with each involuntary swallow. The shuttle
had stabilized, and he could now stand up without fear
of falling over. He shut off the auto-pilot and let it idle
while he stood at the window, looking out at the infinite
expanse before him. To him, each star seemed to be a
potential point of existence that everyone could or
couldn't follow, depending on the hand that guided
them.

For a lucky few, that hand may even be their own.

Choices, he thought, had never been his to make.
He wondered how many of his own decisions were
guided, not by that hand of the infinite abyss, but by the
sneering jowls and yellowed-teeth of those that
programmed the OPT. Even now, it was likely still
clouding his perception despite its tormenting process of
deactivation.

That frightened man, like many before him,
imagined the colonists as disgusting animals who barked

sadistic orders as they watched him and all that he'd ever known deteriorate. In his mind, their skin had changed pigment from decades away from the earth, and they looked more alien than human. Maybe with pallid gray skin and colorless eyes.

Serpents slithered into Jonah's mind, whispering thoughts of revenge and cursing those who had perpetrated his recent sufferings. These thoughts began to call out the guilty and imbued in him a seed that would grow into one of the greater evils of humankind; self-righteous anger.

It was the same thing that the men following Robespierre had thought when they rolled out the guillotine. It was what the Russian revolutionaries thought of when they murdered the royal family down to the smallest child — all well-intentioned, but blind to the dissonance in what they had set out to do.

Jonah felt rage bubbling up from under his skin, and for a few brief moments, he forgot all about the throbbing of his head and the burning in his throat. He let it fill him like an overflowing cup. Relished in it.

With a grimace, he looked at his destination. The moon was not very far, relative to the distance from which he started, and if he were to accelerate, he could be there in less than twenty minutes.

Without warning, he began to scream and punch the window in from of him like some primordial sacrament to appease the fire that threatened to consume him.

Yet, drifting as he was, Jonah seemed like an angry insect that had been captured in a tin-can. Suspended in black amber. His mandibles were futilely clicking, and his arms were unsuccessfully attempting to offset the cruel hand of the child-god that had thoughtlessly placed him there.

That had left him there.

A long and high-pitched beeping interrupted his fit.

He stopped and listened for where the noise might be coming from. It seemed to be coming from the dashboard, a transmission from the colony.

Swinging quickly from futile rage to cautious apprehension, Jonah pushed the blinking button on the console of the shuttle. Suddenly, a mechanical voice began to speak with a monotonous tone and stilted rhythm.

"Hello, shuttle driver. It appears that you are approaching the colony. We appreciate you and how you toil for the greater good, but, unfortunately, there are no scheduled shipments set to arrive today. Please turn around and come back on a scheduled day."

"I need to land," he said to the disembodied voice.

"Hello, shuttle driver. It appears that you are approaching the colony. We…"

"I want to speak to a person *godammit*! Where are you bastards, huh?" Jonah began yelling into the microphone in a futile attempt to speak to someone living. To find a face or an affected voice to sling his curses at. Between his shouts and cries, the machine continued with its "…appears that you are approaching the colony" and "…unfortunately, there are no scheduled shipments…"

Furious, Jonah flipped off the voice and began to fly the shuttle manually toward the lunar colony at full speed. The ship creaked as it leaned forward, and his neck hurt from whiplash caused by the sudden shift of movement.

The man had no experience flying a shuttle, but even he was able to navigate it with relative ease. The manual controls were installed in case of emergencies and, as such, were simply designed. It had been crafted like a steering wheel you could push forward and backward as well as side to side.

He pushed the controls as far forward as possible.

Jonah fell as the ship accelerated further, and he hit his head with a sharp thump on the console in front of him. Blood came trickling down from the point of impact and trailed his face in slow streams of crimson.

Stunned and lightheaded, he tried to stand and felt both his own body and gravity working against him in equal measures. Once he finally did manage to stand upright, he could see that the ship was now very close to the colony, less than a minute from impact if he were to continue at his present speed.

Yet, as he stared at it all, he began to feel that rare sense of understanding that occasionally came to men. Jonah began to understand the damage that he would potentially cause and the suffering that this decision would reckon on those unsuspecting families trying to eke out their sorry existences. Just like him before the last few days happened.

Maybe, he thought, *their hands have been forced as well.*

He then began to feel as though Gray Hills and the lunar colony were more alike than dissimilar. They were both placed in a bubble of sorts, amid a harsh and unforgiving wasteland. Both were deprived, in different ways. He still hated them for what they had done to him and those few that he knew well.

Yet, the thought occurred that his present course wasn't the right course, that this wasn't any answer at all. Fire begets fire. One mishap does not absolve another.

Quickly and as deftly as his disoriented mind would allow, he swung the controls as far to his right as he could. The shuttle's engine rattled loudly and let out a high-pitched whine, and the controls strained as he narrowly missed the giant fist of glass that contained the colony within.

Instead, the shuttle crashed into the gray wasteland

of the moon about a couple miles away from his initial destination. It scraped violently against the cold, pallid tundra of the moon and pivoted from side to side, fishtailing and spinning.

That decision was made in a split second, like the swing of a fast and capricious pendulum. One moment, he had let thoughts of revenge hang like overcast cumulous. The next, he had considered the repercussions that he would have imposed upon so many undeserving lives.

Jonah had known—had been gifted the knowledge —that allowing one moment of anger to determine so much for so many made him no better than the ones who had thrust him into a life of lies (or at best, half-truths).

It made him no better than the man in sackcloth whose words and intentions wove like webs around him, ending somewhere he couldn't hope to see or understand. Nor any better than the dead android who had used him as bait for his attempt at revenge.

Rocks and sediment flew in all directions as the shuttle barreled forward until friction had finally done its invisible work and forced the vehicle to a stop.

A plume of smoke rose slowly from the front of the shuttle, twisting and zigzagging with no atmosphere to hold it in place, floating into the empty vacuum of space. A small fog of dust hovered around the crash site, and the shuttle sat silent. The dust settled back down, but still, there was no movement within.

After several minutes, Jonah finally began to regain consciousness. He had been knocked out on impact. The whole cabin had the fishy, sulfuric smell of overcharged wires and melted plastic. His vision was a blur.

Slowly, like a leaky faucet filling an empty cup, he realized where he was and what had happened. What he had wanted to do and what he had decided to do and why that distinction mattered.

He was still thirsty, and his head throbbed like a bloated timpani. Yet, Jonah was surprised to feel the odd sense of contentment that came over him at that moment. The feeling that he had made the right choice.

Blood from his injury had congealed and formed a sort of arc on both sides of his face. The gas station clerk took a deep breath and tried to compose himself as best as he could.

Jonah slowly and painfully rose to his feet, but the effort was easier than he had anticipated. His whole body felt lighter, like a weight that he had been carrying his whole life had finally been lifted. Was it the reduced gravity?

Downing saw the damaged contours of the shuttle, and his face felt hot. Feral sparks had been flying waywardly from the untethered wires of the console and had burned the exposed areas of his skin while he had been unconscious.

Blistered streaks glistened in the flashing lights of the cabin and, having noticed them, only then began to burn.

So it goes, he thought as he scooted away from the wires and looked at the red blotches of his singed hands.

Using the walls of the ship for support, he made his way to the door and saw encased in the now shattered glass a suit with which he could traverse that harsh new wasteland. For a short time, anyway.

Carefully avoiding the shards of glass, Jonah grabbed the suit and the thin oxygen tank and put them both on as best as he could, reading what he could of the torn instruction manual.

Alighting like a man from the mouth of a silver whale, he jumped from the bent door and slowly fell to the gray ground below. His first footfalls rang hollow and muffled through the empty air around him, but despite this and everything else, he felt optimistic for whatever it was that the future may yet hold for him.

Jonah tried to touch the source of pain from the left side of his head but only touched his helmet instead. He laughed at this. Softly, at first, but then gradually began laughing so loud that his sides hurt. Tears streamed down his face and burned the open wounds they crossed through.

The questions and answers didn't matter much to him now. Jonah Downing focused all his attention on placing one foot in front of the other. *Come what may,* he thought, *because it will come whether or not it's given my humble permission.*

There were craters all around him that looked like deep gray calderas of long-dormant volcanoes. It was both a terrifying and a beautiful sight.

Jonah walked forward, thankful for the reduced gravity that was working in his favor and hoped he didn't have much further to go. But he kept his head down, figuring that the distance would seem shorter if he didn't think about it.

EPILOGUE

Annette sprang up from her mat on the floor. It was called a bed, but that was hardly accurate. It resembled one in only the vaguest manner, with pillows and blankets, both perpetually askew, and a person who regularly slept on it. It was an uncomfortable thing with knotted lumps that dug into her back no matter which position she slept in.

An alarm clock on a small table across from her bed flashed 0800. She'd have the day to herself. At least the first few hours. She was thankful for that. In such a cramped apartment, moments of solitude were commodities that one caught when they could. Little embers of privacy and independence were essential to most of the people on the colony but especially for the young girl who had scarcely known such things. It would be a vacation from the crowded world she had been thrust into and forced to inhabit.

Annette had lived her whole life in the colony. In this same one-room apartment. She'd occasionally have fantasies of a life where they could get a larger one. They were an Echelon-Five family, the lowest of the colony ranks, and were grouped into a massive apartment complex that housed all the other Echelon-Five families.

She had heard from a friend that the Echelon-Fours were given two separate rooms in their apartments, divided by real walls and not the cloth sheets that separated her room from her parents in their own home, but she was doubtful. Often, rumors that sounded too good to be true were too good to be true.

Shuffling onto the cold linoleum floor of the kitchen, she looked from wall to wall. Her unkempt black hair stuck up like a war banner, and her green eyes shone brightly amid the tawny brown of her face. Placed haphazardly on the table in front of her, she found a note scribbled in the untidy script of her mother's hand.

Annie,

I hope you have a good day. Make sure you clean up the house.

Also, your father forgot his lunch and needs you to bring it to him.

Love,
Mom

She heaved a long sigh. This was not how she wanted to start her day, but oh well.

Opening the refrigerator, she pulled out the ration pack marked L for lunches and put it into a cloth lunch bag. At least she'd get to look around the colony, she thought.

Annette left the massive Echelon-Five complex and

began to walk toward the East Gate, where her father was stationed. He was a guard, a door guard, which was why they were only Fives, she thought. Truthfully, she loved both her parents immensely, but when you are the lowest caste in a glass bubble of five-million other people, it can make you resent those around you. No matter how much you love them.

Outside, she passed a long-dried fountain that contained the statue of a large man standing at the center. Annette couldn't recall his name but knew he was one of the 'founders of the colony' or a scientist or something. It was hard containing all the facts people told her were important, but, in the case of the man on the fountain, it was even more difficult. He had been exiled twelve years ago and hadn't been spoken of much since then, aside from the occasional cautionary tales the teachers liked to use to scare the children.

On the stone, faux-marble base of the statue, the plaque had been crudely scratched out. All that remained were the barely decipherable letters of his first and last name: *A* and *S*.

Walking faster now, she hoped to get her errand over with as quickly as possible but was stopped short by the trill of an emergency announcement. All the people living out their lives stopped and listened as the somber, calculated voice of a young woman spoke to the whole colony.

Attention, Attention! Please be on your guard. A shuttle has been stolen from our support town of Gray Hills and has crashed not far from the east gate. Do not panic, as our guards have been trained in how to handle this situation, but beware of any person you do not recognize. Attention, Attention!

Annette's heart felt like a stone sinking to the bottom of her chest. "Dad's at the east gate," she muttered to herself and began to run now. As fast as she could.

Her father was a tall, dark-skinned man with round glasses and a lean face. He was in a frantic conversation with two of the other guards when he stopped mid-sentence to address his daughter, out of breath and panting.

"Annie, what are you doing here? Didn't you hear the announcement?" His voice was stern and filled with worry.

"I'm sorry, Dad. Mom left a note telling me to bring you your lunch, and when I heard the announcement, I was already almost here," she said while averting her bright eyes from his hard ones.

"Dammit," he said to himself. "Well, there's not much we can do about it now. Just turn around and go back home. And don't forget to lock the…"

"Carson?" said one of the guards, addressing her father.

"What is it? Can't you see I'm talking to my daughter?!" he said sharply.

"I know, but it's important. The man—the defector —he's here. Approaching the gate now." The guard who spoke was a slight woman, meek in frame and personality. She was shaking with fear.

Carson's eyes widened, and he looked out onto the pale landscape and cursed again. "Annette, you've got to go. Now!"

"But Dad…" she tried.

"Go!" he said, voice harsh with fear as he turned to look out the window of the gate at the man approaching.

The man was clad in a spacesuit and awkwardly walking as if he was injured or dazed. His path was not straight, but he wasn't far from the gate now, and the guard had to be prepared for anything.

People could be deceptive.

They had all heard the stories of what happened

twelve years ago, after all. That cautionary tale was not just for the children of the colony.

He counted back from ten, a calming technique, and kept his trembling hand on the stun gun at his side.

Annette was terrified but curious as well. She had run a few steps ahead at the bark of her father's voice, yet she felt the compulsion to stop and look back.

The young girl saw an approaching astronaut, only for an instant, staggering as he approached. His glass helmet was haloed in the blue light of the earth. It reflected brightly like a flare.

As far back as Annette could remember, she had been warned that people from below may try to take their homes away, that they may destroy the lives they had worked so hard to build. To steal it for themselves.

But, she thought, *what if that's not true?* She'd heard the broadcasts, listened to her father and her teachers. Yet, those from Gray Hills never got a chance to speak for themselves. That didn't seem right.

Her father yelled at her to go once again. She wanted to stay, to see who it was and talk to them. Ask questions about what it was like down there, the world her father had come from.

But, she couldn't help feeling the fear creeping into her body now. It was brought on by the worried look on the faces of those gathered around her. In the grating fear in her father's voice.

So she turned around, ran the whole way home without stopping or looking back, and locked the door behind her.

Acknowledgments

There are a lot of people who've helped support and guide me on my path, and I'll try my best to name them all.

Thank you, Carolyn, my beautiful wife, for the love and support that allows me to carry on with every whim that possesses my mind.

Thank you, Anastasia, the light of my life, and the greatest daughter a father could ever hope to have. You help me see the world in ways I had long forgotten, and you have given my life the highest purpose imaginable.

Thank you, Ridge, for listening to my ideas and supporting these concepts when they were still the garbled mess that had yet to be articulated from thought to page. Thank you for reading my drafts and the final story and for your honest critiques. They mean the world to me.

Thank you to all my other friends, especially my brother and best friend, Anthony McLaughlin, for your intelligence and support in all things artistic that I've been inclined to follow these past twenty years with you.

Thank you, Mom and Dad, for supporting me in my writing, even when I was young. I won't lie and say our relationship has ever been perfect, mainly when we lived under the same roof, but the good things persist.

Thank you to my teachers, both college and before, who pushed me and told me to stop procrastinating. I never followed through with that advice, but I appreciate it just the same.

Lastly, I'd like to thank Violet Ladd. You fostered my love for books and fantasies back when I was just a boy. I miss you dearly, and though I'm not inclined to believe in any kind of afterlife, I hope that you stand beside the throne of the God you loved so much, draped in the eternal love you deserve.

Made in the USA
San Bernardino, CA
07 February 2020